Praise for Harry and Rebecca:

'I read it to my sons and
we laughed ourselves inside out.'
Ed Byrne

'A lovely book that was hard to put down!
Mesmerizing and funny, and
reminded me of Lemony Snicket.'
Ama, age 7, *Toppsta*

'Children may find their bedside table raided by
parents eager to get aboard the laugh-train!'
**Jesse Armstrong (writer of *Peep Show*,
Succession, *Four Lions*)**

'An absolutely thrilling adventure!'
Spirited, age 7, *Toppsta*

'Captivating illustrations.
Children . . . are likely to be enthralled.'
Children's Books Ireland

'A great adventure book.'
Simon, age 6, *Toppsta*

FABER has published children's books since 1929. T. S. Eliot's *Old Possum's Book of Practical Cats* and Ted Hughes' *The Iron Man* were amongst the first. Our catalogue at the time said that 'it is by reading such books that children learn the difference between the shoddy and the genuine'. We still believe in the power of reading to transform children's lives. All our books are chosen with the express intention of growing a love of reading, a thirst for knowledge and to cultivate empathy. We pride ourselves on responsible editing. Last but not least, we believe in kind and inclusive books in which all children feel represented and important.

HARRY HEAPE is an artist, a visionary and a very successful none-of-your-businessman. A shy and quiet man, Harry lives and writes on the edge of a magical forest where he spends any spare time that he has collecting enamel badges.

REBECCA BAGLEY lives in Bath (the city, not A BATH, although she did have one once) where she draws pictures so she doesn't have to get a real job. When she's not hanging out in the world of children's books, she'll probably be in a headstand, plotting how best to smuggle a husky into her flat without anyone noticing.

Indiana
Bones
and the LOST Library

Illustrated by

HARRY HEAPE   REBECCA BAGLEY

faber

First published in the UK in 2022
First published in the US in 2022
by Faber and Faber Limited
Bloomsbury House,
74–77 Great Russell Street,
London WC1B 3DA
faberchildrens.co.uk

Typeset in Amaranth by M Rules
This font has been specially chosen to support reading

Printed and bound by
CPI Group (UK) Ltd, Croydon CR0 4YY

A CIP record for this book
is available from the British Library

ISBN 978–0–571–35352–1

FSC
www.fsc.org
MIX
Paper from
responsible sources
FSC® C171272

1 3 5 7 9 10 8 6 4 2

For Henry

King of the Upstairs Upstairs

from your friend H.H. x

Prologue

Hello! ~~Hairy Hippo~~ Harry Heape here! Welcome back to the wonderful world of Indiana Bones and his number one side-pal, Aisha Ghatak. You remember these two heroes, right? Of course you diddley-do.

Indiana Bones is the dog (obvi) and what you need to know about him is that he's a shaggy, magical talking pooch from another

dimension with a fiendish fondness for fish fingers.

What you need to know about Aisha is that she has a black belt in archaeology, she's as clever as a cupcake and brave as a Bengal tiger.

Before we get cracking, I thought it was slimportant to write a 'Reminderoony Section' all about these two and their search for the lost treasure of the Lonely Avenger.

Check it:

- The Lonely Avenger was a French knight who lived more than two thousand years ago.
- He fell in love with King Guntram's daughter, Diane.

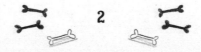

- She was forced to marry Philippe of Castile, a Spanish prince, but he banished her to far-flung lands when she had a daughter because the big foolish fool wanted a son (what a bum-hat).
- The Lonely Avenger pillaged the whole world for treasure to build a shrine to his beloved Diane.
- The treasure has never been found, but Aisha and Bones got super close in the last book.
- Baddies are on their trail: Philip Castle, Lord Henry Lupton (known as the Serpent) and their minion, stinky Ringo.

Philip Castle is a direct descendant of Philippe of Castile, the Spanish prince, and is hell-bent on finding the treasure, so he can reclaim the riches he feels are his birthright. Lupton is a rich and slippery collector who wants the Avenger's treasure because he is greedy and selfish. Ringo is their fool and he smells more frightful than bin juice.

That's enough blah blah blah for now because I am itching to get into the story because it's a great big banger.

Okay. Let's bounce.

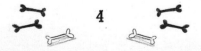

1

Back to Earth

It was a deliciously soft summer's morning and the whole world was as quiet as a library for moths. Aisha and Julimus drifted gently down through the creamy clouds in their wonderful, but now rather battered, tuk-tuk hot air balloon, made especially for them in

a motorbike repair shop in the backstreets of Casablanca. They were both zonked and very much looking forward to a mega-snoozzze.

Our valiant voyagers sat slumped in silence. They were returning from an epic badventure which had culminated in an escape from a pyramid, followed by a scarifying rescue from the Egyptian army, the Serpent and Castle. They had met Julimus on their travels and had helped him free his son from a curse deep within the tummy of one of the pyramids. Worried that the baddies knew where Aisha and Indiana lived, Julimus had invited his new friends to stay at his house. It was little wonder they were pooped and more than happy to sit in peace, with Aisha's dog Indiana

Bones and Julimus's boy Jovis curled up asleep under a thick Persian blanket.

The shabby-suited Julimus checked his maps and announced, 'By my calculations, we should be close. It is time to drop through the clouds and see whether I am correct. Forgive me if we are in fact right above a volcano!' he joked.

Julimus skilfully steered the balloon lower, through the mist. Aisha peered down, excited to see where they would plop out.

If she had been a cartoon, her eyes would have boinged out on springs because as they emerged from the clouds, Aisha saw that they were directly above the River Thames, over central London, heading down towards Tower Bridge.

Aisha woke Indiana Bones and the boy Jovis, knowing they wouldn't want to miss the excitement of floating serenely above somewhere that very much felt like home.

'Yay!' said Indiana Bones. 'Londinium! Let's get some fish and chips,' he added, rubbing his belly and licking his lips.

Julimus brought them lower, and they passed right between the two towers of Tower Bridge. Passengers on a red London bus, stuck in morning traffic, looked up, surprised. A gang of school children waved, clapped and took photos. A city gentleman raised his bowler hat to them as a greeting. It's not every day that you see a floating tuk-tuk hot air balloon cruising above the Thames.

The Good Team floated serenely on, towards the Tower of London on the banks of the river. 'That is the home of the Crown Jewels,' Julimus informed them, nodding knowledgeably towards the medieval fortress. Aisha's heart skipped a beat, as it always did when she heard about yummy treasure. It reminded her about the vast, swaggy piles of loot that the Avenger had hidden somewhere.

Just days ago, she and Indiana had felt sure that they were on the cusp of finding it in the Great Pyramid of Khufu. Instead, they found an empty coffin, the Avenger's silver sword and, thrillingly, his journal, which Aisha hoped would give them plenty of clues as to where to look next for the French knight's fortune. Even

better, their deadly enemies didn't know of the journal's existence.

The tuk-tuk floated past St Katharine Docks and Indiana's super-keen doggy ears picked up the buzz of a light aircraft somewhere above them. He lifted his sunglasses and peered into the heavens.

'Nearly home,' declared Julimus.

'I can't wait to see where you live,' replied Aisha.

'Don't get too excited,' said Julimus. 'It is a very modest apartment that comes with my other job. Archaeology doesn't always pay well and so I also work as a school caretaker—' He broke off and pointed. 'Look! St Paul's Cathedral!'

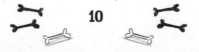

As they headed towards Westminster Bridge, Julimus and Aisha too became aware of the noise of the aircraft Indiana had picked up moments earlier. *I smell trouble*, Indiana thought to himself, sniffing at the sky.

'We have company,' he announced. 'Small seaplane. Looks as though it could carry half a dozen people. Could be heading our way.'

'Why do I get the feeling we're being followed?' Aisha asked anxiously, hoping Julimus would tell her that seaplanes were common above the Thames and there was no need to worry. As they watched, the plane arced and began to head quite clearly towards them.

'I feel the same way,' Julimus replied, trying in vain to increase the speed of the hot air balloon.

'There's no way we're outrunning anything in this,' Aisha said. 'I just hope we can make it to your house before they catch us up.'

'If Ringo or the Serpent or Castle is in that plane, I am going to be as grumpy as a camel with a bum splinter,' said Indiana indignantly.

'They may try to force us down onto the river,' Julimus fretted. 'I'm going to take us away from the water.' He turned the tuk-tuk's handlebars and headed north. They scooted over Buckingham Palace and London Zoo, edging towards the safety of his home.

As they neared their destination, the

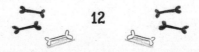

seaplane began to climb higher into the sky, which made our friends feel a little safer.

'Seems as though we may have been getting panicky for nothing,' said Julimus. 'They look to be heading up, up and away.'

Just then Jovis stood up and pointed excitedly. 'Home!' he said.

Ahead of them was an old green-roofed Victorian building. As they got closer, Aisha saw that it was a school with a small playground. As they got nearer still, she realised there was an Astroturf football pitch on its flat roof, and gleaming white goalposts with nets at either end. 'Cool!' grinned Indiana. 'Your home has a big green Wembley wig on!'

Julimus brought the tired and battered hot

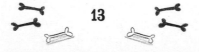

air balloon smoothly down to land, right in the centre of the pitch. The crew clambered out and stretched their aching bodies, thinking how delicious it would be to finally get some proper rest.

These feelings of happiness were to last but a second as, from behind his trademark sunglasses, Indiana looked up into the sky and saw the seaplane again, now circling high above. To their alarm, two tiny figures in black jumped out of the plane. Within a few short seconds, they'd pulled open parachutes and were floating silently down towards the friends.

'Oh dearie measles,' gulped Julimus. 'But how did they find us?'

'But I'm as tired as ten teenage tortoises,' grumbled Indiana. 'Sleepy as a sloth. I'm more worn out than a shuffler's shoe.'

'They can land right next to me. I don't care,' sighed Aisha. 'I shall curl up and sleep at their feet. They can talk to me tomorrow.'

Shielding their eyes against the sun, the four friends watched the figures descend. The strangers were both wearing balaclavas. Whoever they were, whether it was the Serpent, Castle or smelly Ringo, there would be no more running.

As the intruders came in to land, Aisha, Julimus and Jovis slowly backed away, and Indiana got ready to defend the group.

The figures in black touched down skilfully.

In a super-smooth manoeuvre, the taller of the two unclipped his parachute. Walking towards them, he slowly pulled off his balaclava to reveal shoulder-length grey hair and a kind, twinkly face.

Aisha's heart boomed. 'Dad!' she bellowed, and she and Indiana sprinted towards him, both feeling happier than a pair of chubby butt cheeks in a pants shop.

Dr Satnam Ghatak lost his balance as the pair jumped at him, falling backwards onto the pretend grass. Aisha hugged her dad for all she was worth and Indiana licked him like a lollipop, all over his friendly face. Aisha hadn't seen her world-famous archaeologist dad for weeks. In fact, he'd been locked up, yet again,

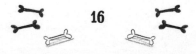

in a far-flung country for digging somewhere without the correct paperwork. He hugged Aisha long and hard and kissed her four times on the forehead. It felt wonderful!

Finally, Dr Ghatak stood up, twinkling. 'I hear you've been having the most splendid time in Egypt!' he started, but was immediately silenced as Indiana bounced all over him again.

'Lovely to see you too, my boy!' he laughed in between enormous doggy kisses. 'But do let me get up. There's someone I need to introduce you to.'

In their joy, Aisha and Indiana had forgotten that two people had landed on the roof. Turning, they saw the second figure walking towards them, removing her balaclava.

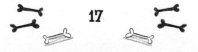

She was a woman with shoulder-length blonde hair, which she ruffled and ran her fingers through.

'This is my friend Celia Kane,' Dr Ghatak announced with a very big smile. 'Celia works for an insurance company. She's a sort of loss adjuster.'

Everyone said their hellos and then Julimus led them all inside. Even though it was warm, Aisha felt distinctly chilly. She had so much to tell her dad and she wished very much that she could have him all to herself.

As Indiana trotted in behind Aisha and her dad, he began wondering about his own mother and father, something he hadn't done for a while. He couldn't remember his parents. Our

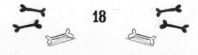

special hero knew he'd once lived in Skara Brae in the far north of Scotland, thousands of years ago. Dr Ghatak had found him as a pup, in a magical underground chamber, frozen in time.

He adored Aisha's father and was sure his own mum and dad would have loved his new family too. But he did wish he'd been able to get to know his parents before settling down as the Ghataks' family pet.

While he pondered, the marvellous and mysterious sapphire in Indiana's collar began to change colour, glowing slightly at the memory of where he was from.

2

Eyes in the Sky

Aisha's brainbox was buzzing like a wonky old robot. Her mind had a million thoughts, all jostling for space. She longed to tell her father everything and was dying to look through the journal with him, to see if they could find clues as to where to look next for the lost treasure.

However, wherever her father was, Celia was never far behind, so for now, Aisha was not sharing any secrets.

They all sat in Julimus's kitchen, and the mood felt awkward. 'How did you find us so quickly?' Julimus asked Dr Ghatak.

'As soon as I was released, I rang Edith,' Dr Ghatak replied. 'She told me you'd been in Egypt on an epic adventure and that you were all heading back here for a bit of rest and recuperation.'

'I lent Satnam some money to hire the seaplane and here we are!' chipped in Celia.

Aisha looked at Celia. 'How much does it cost to hire a seaplane?' she asked.

'Not as much as you might think,' Celia

answered without actually telling her. 'When I helped Satnam get out of jail in Darmak, we were rather stuck getting home, and so I just thought, why not hire a seaplane? You only live once!'

Dr Ghatak smiled. 'I appreciate it and I will pay you back.'

Aisha decided that something about Celia didn't add up. She had been visiting Charman and Dukes, the travel agents, with her father for as long as she could remember and she knew that hiring a seaplane and a pilot would cost many thousands of pounds. It seemed a lot of money for someone who worked in insurance. Aisha looked down at Indiana Bones and noticed the sapphire in his collar

pulsing softly, meaning his magic was at work. Perhaps he too felt something was not quite right with Dr Ghatak's new friend. He was certainly keeping his magic chatty gift a secret for the time being. As this was always difficult for him, he'd slunk off to the sofa for a sneaky siesta.

Julimus was bustling about, keen to be the perfect host. 'Satnam, Celia, you are my guests here, and you are most welcome. Let me show you around.' Unfortunately, in the kitchen Julimus was embarrassed to find he did not have much food to share with his friends.

'Don't worry,' said Celia. 'As we are imposing on you, I insist on making supper tonight! I shall go and buy ingredients for a

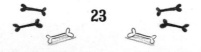

23

meal. What else do you need for the house? It's on me.'

'That sounds wonderful,' agreed Dr Ghatak. 'Do let us pay our way.'

Julimus was tired and this sounded good. 'That is very kind, thank you,' he replied. Aisha sloped off to the sofa for an Indiana cuddle, while Celia and Julimus made a shopping list.

As soon as Celia had headed out to the shops, Aisha jumped up and pulled Dr Ghatak aside. 'Dad,' she pleaded, 'I need to talk to you.' She ushered him into Julimus's tiny bathroom and locked the door.

Words began to cascade out of her. She told him all about:

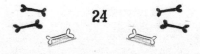

- The steamship *Angel*
- Casablanca
- The Egyptian sandstorm
- Their journey to the pyramids
- The search for the lost treasure of the Lonely Avenger deep in the belly of the pyramid
- *And much, much more.*

Dr Ghatak listened intently, beaming at his beloved girl. 'You seem like you have been very close to striking gold, my dear!' he grinned, the moment there was a pause in Aisha's chitter-chatter. 'I am so proud of you. We will have plenty of time to catch up over the next few days, but now we're all really hungry. Celia

makes the most delicious spaghetti puttanesca. She's keen to get to know you.'

Later, while Celia and Dr Ghatak cooked together in Julimus's small kitchen, Aisha told them everything, from the moment they met Julimus and began their journey around the world, to the thrilling escape from the Egyptian soldiers. She told them all about the baddies – Philip Castle and the vile, wealthy Serpent, Lord Henry Lupton.

Celia looked up from the sauce she was stirring. 'Did you say Lupton?' she asked.

'Yes,' Aisha said. 'Do you know him?' But Celia didn't answer. Instead, she took off her apron and disappeared into another room. Moments later, she returned, talking on the

phone, with her handbag and coat.

Finishing her call, she announced, 'Change of plan, Satnam. Something's come up. You finish supper – I'll see you all later.'

And with that she was gone, leaving Aisha and Indiana staring after her.

The puttanesca that Celia started to make but didn't finish was delicious. With Dr Ghatak's new friend out for the evening, our magical scruffy dog from Skara Brae was able to chat freely. He enjoyed sucking the spaghetti into his mouth as loudly as possible and making himself go cross-eyed while he slurped, which got them all giggling.

By the time they'd all had seconds and cleaned their plates, Dr Ghatak could see Aisha

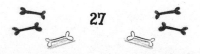

needed to have some real rest. He carried her into Jovis's room and tucked her in the bottom bunk. Indiana and Jovis were curled up together on the top bunk, where Indiana was already dreaming about introducing the wonders of marshmallows and candy floss to his mum and dad in Skara Brae.

Before retiring themselves, Dr Ghatak and Julimus each had a cup of chai. Dr Ghatak made it on the stove, like his mother did, mixing a cinnamon stick and cardamom into the milky tea. They stood out on the flat roof and looked across the twinkly London skyline. Aisha's dad thanked his old friend for looking after his daughter, which made the shabby-suited man smile.

'Ha, she looked after me much more!' he replied. 'She returned Jovis to me, and that incredible dog of yours saved my boy's life, both of which are longer stories I will tell you when it is not so late.'

'They're quite a pair,' agreed Dr Ghatak. 'It is splendid to see you, Julimus. I hope you don't mind us staying a couple of days.'

'Your home is my home, Satnam,' his old friend replied, gazing out across the city.

'Are you working on anything interesting?' Dr Ghatak enquired.

'Well, as a matter of fact, I am,' replied Julimus, smiling softly. 'My caretaking job at the school is very flexible and so I have plenty of time for archaeology. I've been working

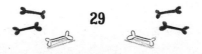

with the British Museum. They have the most excellent piece of technology that uses 3D imagery, rather like a big X-ray machine. I have been using it to look inside the tummies of Egyptian mummies.'

'Wow!' said Dr Ghatak. 'Very good. A machine from the future to unlock the secrets of the past!'

While the friends were chatting, two things of interest were happening in the city below them. The mysterious Celia was whizzing alongside the River Thames on a motorbike. And a mile away, across town, unpleasant things were bubbling in a gherkin-shaped building.

On the thirteenth floor of this building was

an office, and in that office a well-dressed Henry Lupton was plotting. He sat at a slick bank of computer screens, typing carefully, using a mouse to move images around. This slithery Serpent was building up a record of everything he knew about the Ghataks, their weird, annoying hound, and the unknown man in the shabby brown suit.

A phone buzzed. The Serpent picked up the receiver, hissing, 'Send them in.' Moments later a door silently slid open and in walked Philip Castle with his scruffy goon, Ringo.

'Useless fools!' the Serpent spat, turning to glare at his visitors. 'Would either of you care to explain to me why we are always one step behind a child and a stupid dog?' he bellowed,

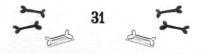

throwing an empty teacup at them, which smashed on the wall behind.

Philip Castle shot Ringo a dirty look as the Serpent fumed, 'No? I'll tell you then! They've been smarter, quicker and braver than you every step of the way, and they're still miles ahead in the search for the Avenger's treasure.'

'Where *do* they get their information from?' Castle asked nervously.

'UNLIKE YOU, THEY ARE PROFESSIONALS!' The Serpent bubbled and boiled, unable to contain his anger. 'I have had Dr Ghatak followed for months. He is a world-renowned archaeologist, his daughter is clever and tenacious, and their horrible hound is incredible. It's like he's possessed! He ran rings

around us all in Egypt – he was too much for twenty soldiers! THAT. IS. NOT. NORMAL.'

Castle and Ringo shifted uneasily, like a pair of children, as the Serpent regained his composure. 'They are a formidable team, make no mistake about it. However, we are on to them,' he added, bringing up on screen an image taken earlier that day.

'Look what I have discovered while you two snored and grunted under your disgusting duvets,' Lupton said.

'I don't snore,' said Castle, keen not to be tarred with the same brush as his smelly associate.

Lupton continued: 'There were numerous sightings of their balloon over London.

This picture was taken from a bus on London Bridge.'

Ringo picked his nose and tried to think of something to say, but his mind was emptier than Mother Hubbard's sweetie jar.

'Have there been sightings outside of London?' Castle asked keenly, stepping closer to the monitors.

'There have not,' said Lupton. 'It is reasonable to assume that they are still in the capital. I have eyes and ears all over the city. It won't be long before we find out exactly where they are.'

'So, we bide our time and then pounce?' ventured Castle, trying to sound as cool as cucumber ice cream.

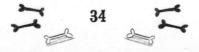

'No,' replied the Serpent. 'I plan to be one step ahead of them, for a change.'

Lupton typed speedily, bringing up new information. 'Here are Dr Ghatak's phone records. There were several calls from Darmak, including one to a company that hired out a seaplane and a pilot. There were two passengers – Ghatak and one other.'

'Do we know who it was?' Castle asked.

'No,' Lupton replied, looking at the screen. 'No other information – yet.'

'Safe to assume they could be just as dangerous as the Ghataks,' said Castle, scratching his stubbly chin.

The Serpent nodded. 'There is a surprising lack of any other travel arrangements. Which

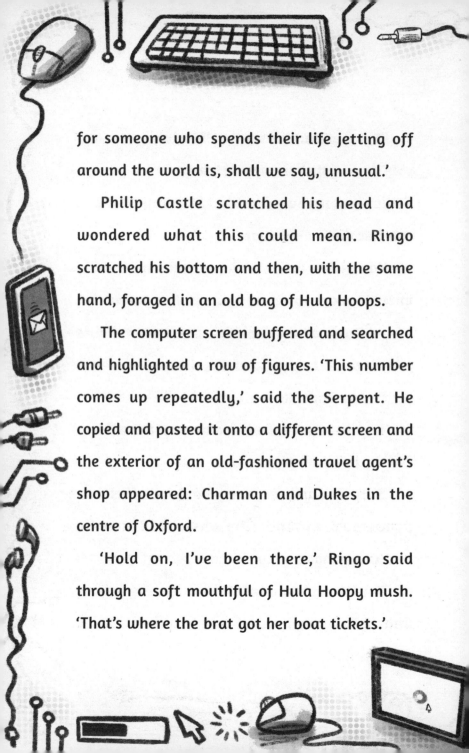

for someone who spends their life jetting off around the world is, shall we say, unusual.'

Philip Castle scratched his head and wondered what this could mean. Ringo scratched his bottom and then, with the same hand, foraged in an old bag of Hula Hoops.

The computer screen buffered and searched and highlighted a row of figures. 'This number comes up repeatedly,' said the Serpent. He copied and pasted it onto a different screen and the exterior of an old-fashioned travel agent's shop appeared: Charman and Dukes in the centre of Oxford.

'Hold on, I've been there,' Ringo said through a soft mouthful of Hula Hoopy mush. 'That's where the brat got her boat tickets.'

'Can you hack into that shop?' asked Castle.

'This is the same technology used by the British government,' the Serpent responded. 'I can hack into anywhere.'

He clicked and dragged and typed and entered reams of code into his supercomputer, but this time none of his tricks worked. He leaned back, exasperated. 'Nothing. Well, that's a first,' he frowned.

'I guess you can't hack into *anywhere*,' Castle dared to say.

'Yes. I. Can.' The Serpent shot Castle a furious look. 'What this means is that Charman and Dukes have no online presence at all.'

A picture appeared on a screen of Mr Charman and Mr Dukes. It was from a

newspaper article entitled 'The Elderly Gentlemen of Travel'.

'Looking at them, you can see why they are not on the internet,' the Serpent sneered. 'They must have a combined age of nearly three thousand. The furthest these two have gone in terms of technology is the telephone.'

'We could give them a ring,' suggested Ringo.

'*Estúpido idiota!* Obviously, we're not going to give them a ring,' growled Castle.

'I am going to do something tremendous and very clever,' hissed the Serpent.

'What?' asked Ringo nervously.

'I am going to place an electronic tap on the phone line of this Charman and Dukes.'

The Serpent dragged and clicked and

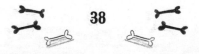

moments later an icon appeared in the bottom corner of one of the screens.

PHONE TAP SECURED

'There,' said the Serpent. 'Simple. As soon as Ghatak or anyone else makes contact, we shall listen. The moment they decide to venture anywhere, we shall know. For once, we shall be one step ahead of them. And then we will strike faster than poop through a Gloucestershire goose.'

3

The Journal

The next morning our heroes were enjoying the most enormous lie-in the history of all lie-ins. Aisha and Indiana had slept the sleep of seventy-seven sleepy sleepers, Aisha dreaming of treasure and Indiana of Skara Brae. Both enjoyed their dreams and woke the next morning feeling totally warm, safe and happy, like robots whose batteries were now at 100 per cent.

Dr Ghatak and Celia had popped out early and returned with some delicious pastries. Dr Ghatak thought that a happy family breakfast in the morning sunshine was just what was needed. Aisha was outside drinking tea at a table, beneath a large stripy umbrella. Indiana had his sunglasses on and was sipping the final section of a mango lassi very noisily through a wiggly straw. Julimus and Jovis were on the football pitch, where the small boy was taking penalties against his dad.

Celia went inside to warm the pastries. Aisha leaned in and whispered to Indiana, 'Who

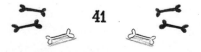

even is she? Celia? Is she his girlfriend? If so, what does that even mean?'

'I don't know,' Indiana whispered back. 'I'm not sure about her. She smells of danger and fibs.'

'Dad said she was a loss adjuster for an insurance company, whatever that is,' said Aisha. 'She's as fishy as a fish tank if you ask me. I always thought Dad would go for someone more exciting, like a mountaineer or an Olympic skateboarder.'

'Confirmative,' agreed Bones, slurping at his empty glass.

'I wish she was the owner of a theme park,' said Aisha, grinning at Indiana. 'Or the world's biggest ice cream shop!'

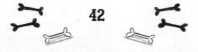

'What are you two chatting about?' said Dr Ghatak, walking over and sitting down.

'Dream jobs,' replied Indiana quickly, 'and Aisha's obsession with ice cream.'

Celia joined them at the table with the warm pastries, causing Indiana to clamp his jaw shut. They sat in strained silence for a few awkward minutes, which in truth felt like hours.

'Well ... this is all very ... nice,' said Dr Ghatak, trying to paper over the cracks of the uncomfortable moment.

'I'll put the kettle on,' said Celia, as if she hadn't noticed. She got up and went back inside.

'You're unusually quiet,' said Dr Ghatak to his daughter.

Aisha didn't know what to say, until she remembered something that both she and her father would be really interested in. 'Ah, Dad, I have something great to show you!' she beamed excitedly. She rushed inside and returned quickly with her backpack, which she unzipped and proceeded to pull out a large, carefully wrapped package. Although she had told her father about their adventures the night before, she hadn't yet shown him the journal. With Celia elsewhere, it was a good time to present her latest archaeological discovery.

'Something from your travels?' her father twinkled, his nostrils flaring. 'Hurry up, my dear! Let's see.'

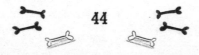

'It's something Jovis found inside the tomb of the Lonely Avenger,' explained Aisha, careful that the little boy received due credit.

Jovis stopped kicking his ball around and joined them at the table, followed by Julimus.

Aisha put on a pair of latex gloves. 'I've been calling this the Avenger's journal,' she explained. 'Although I think it's also a collection of drawings.' She lifted the ancient book out of its protective packaging and held it for her father to examine. 'I was hoping it might provide us with some clues of where to look next for the treasure,' she added.

Dr Ghatak also put on a pair of latex gloves, while Julimus cleared a space at the table and covered it with a protective

polythene sheet. Aisha placed the fragile book on the table and began to unwrap it.

Dr Ghatak nearly fell off his chair when he saw it properly. 'My goodness!' he exclaimed. 'It has the mark of the Avenger on the cover! Jovis, this must be more than two thousand years old, you clever, clever boy.'

Jovis beamed, feeling like a superstar, suddenly a bit awkward and self-conscious. Julimus put a proud and steadying hand on his shoulder.

'Two thousand years old! Wow!' gasped

Aisha. 'Of course. I guess it must be. We were just so relieved to get out of Egypt, I hadn't really thought about it,' she added, embarrassed.

'If this is as old as I think it is, what you have found is one of the greatest archaeological discoveries of the century. It could even be the oldest book ever found and, as such, it is priceless! Stand back – we shouldn't even be breathing next to this book, and it certainly shouldn't be in sunlight.'

A stunned silence descended. 'We do need to look through it though, Dad,' said Aisha.

'Absolutely not,' said Dr Ghatak. 'It's too fragile. A book like this must be preserved at all costs.'

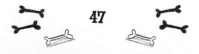

Aisha's eyes narrowed. She felt as angry as a wasp. 'No way are we just wrapping it up and putting it away again. The Avenger left it for me. I have to look through it!' she insisted.

'I don't think that you understand the importance of what you have found,' Dr Ghatak said icily.

'No, I don't think *you* understand the importance of what *we* have found,' countered Aisha, her eyes filling with tears. 'It's our only clue.'

This was a first. Aisha and her father usually agreed on everything. Aisha was not used to being at odds with her dad, and it did not feel good at all.

Julimus realised he needed to act to ease

the tension, before someone said something they would really regret. Speaking directly to the journal, he said, 'How about I wrap you up very carefully for safe keeping, and tomorrow I will take you to the British Museum.'

Aisha glared at Julimus, and then was puzzled as he gave her the gentlest of little winks behind her dad's back. Aisha had no clue what this subtle signal meant and stared after him, open-mouthed, as he slipped away, cradling the Avenger's journal.

'Well ... okay, good!' shouted Dr Ghatak to the departing Julimus. 'The British Museum is just the place for a book of that importance. I shall email my contact there this afternoon.'

It was at this point that Celia reappeared, carrying a tray of coffees. Indiana sniffed gently at the air around her. Whoever she was, she certainly had a knack for slipping in and out unnoticed, he thought.

'What have I missed? Anything fun?' Celia asked.

The atmosphere between Aisha and her father was as icy as an iceberg's armpit. Aisha was still angry and, not wanting to burst into tears, she ran inside. Indiana thought about following her, but stopped himself. He decided that what Aisha needed right now was time to cool down.

The rest of the day was miserable. In the afternoon, Indiana Bones and Jovis played

football, but Aisha was not really in the mood to kick a ball. With her batteries still on 99 per cent, she was aching like a billy goat to get started on the next stage of their hunt for the Avenger's treasure. Wandering back inside, she could hear her father and Celia laughing in the sitting room. Aisha had no desire to go and join them, so she ducked into the kitchen. She still couldn't believe she was forbidden to study the journal, which would soon be beyond her reach in the British Museum. They were as far away from the lost treasure as they had ever been.

Aisha spent the whole of dinner feeling annoyed. She was not hungry and pushed her food around her plate, while Dr Ghatak and

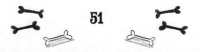

Celia laughed and joked together, behaving as if no one else was there.

When at last her father and Celia went outside for some fresh air, Aisha finally had an opportunity to question Julimus. 'Where's the journal?' she asked.

'It's in a cool box in the hall, ready to take to the British Museum tomorrow,' he told her. 'They have a secure storage room for fragile artefacts. The temperature and humidity are carefully controlled. The journal will be quite safe.'

Aisha looked towards the hall. There indeed was the stripy plastic cool box, the kind you might use for a picnic. This was too tempting for Aisha, who darted over and knelt beside the box, Indiana at her side.

'Should we?' Aisha asked her hairy pal.

'I don't know,' replied Indiana. 'Your dad was pretty clear that we shouldn't, but maybe just a little peek ...?'

The moment that Aisha was about to lift the lid, she looked up and saw her father returning from outside. Their eyes locked along the hall. The smile dropped from his face and Aisha knew that he was seriously angry.

'Aisha,' said Dr Ghatak, 'the answer was no this afternoon, it is a medium-sized **no** now, and it will be an even bigger **no** tomorrow. And do not ask Julimus for help either!' he added, spotting his old friend hovering in the kitchen.

Julimus, stuck in the middle, raised his

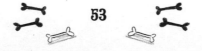

eyebrows and seemed about to speak, but Dr Ghatak was adamant. 'I know that look, Julimus, and it's a no to you as well. I want you to give me your solemn word that you will not allow Aisha anywhere near that priceless book. Promise?'

As Aisha looked at Julimus, she could tell that he was turning something over in his mind before finally replying, 'You have my solemn word. I shall not let Aisha within a mile of the journal.'

Aisha's heart sank. That was that. Julimus had promised and her friend was, above all, a man of honour. Deflated and defeated, Aisha went off to bed, where she tossed and turned and complained to Indiana about how rotten and unfair life was.

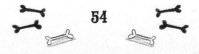

A little later Julimus popped his head around the door. 'Two things,' he whispered. 'Number one, write down your email address.' He passed her a scrap of paper.

'Why?' Aisha asked, scribbling on the paper grumpily. 'Are we going to be penpals now?'

'In a way we are!' said Julimus mysteriously, trying to keep the atmosphere light.

'And the second thing?' Aisha asked.

'The second thing is not to worry,' he said. 'I have left a pile of books you may be interested in if you can't sleep.' He smiled, before slinking out once more.

Aisha, of course, couldn't sleep. Her mind felt like a waterfall with a million questions tumbling down, down, down, followed by a

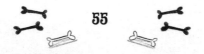

million more. There was no way she was going to nod off.

'Will you quit your fidgeting,' said Indiana, who was always ready for a sneaky snooze.

'I can't stop thinking about the journal and the Serpent and the treasure,' she said. 'We were so close and now I don't know what to do.'

'Count sheep, read a book, anything,' grumped Indiana, pulling a pillow over his head.

Aisha got out of bed, walked over to the pile of books Julimus had left and began to read the titles. One in particular caught her eye: *Alexandria to the Pyramids, an Archaeological Journey.* She picked it up and

snuck back to read it by the light of a small bedside lamp.

There was a map at the beginning of the book. Aisha studied it and pondered the Avenger's journey from Europe. He would have landed at the Mediterranean port of Alexandria and moored his ship, the *Black Tiger*, there. Maybe he stayed a few days. She read about Alexandria. More than two thousand years ago, it was home to an enormous lighthouse, one of the Seven Wonders of the Ancient World.

Aisha's father had told her countless stories about these famous archaeological sites. The Seven Wonders were considered to be the most remarkable buildings or constructions of the ancient world. They included tombs and

temples, glorious gardens and statues which stretched to the sky. The Egyptian pyramids were the best known, and also the only one of the Seven Wonders that had survived to this day. Aisha envied the Lonely Avenger, who would have seen the great lighthouse at Alexandria and the pyramids in their full glory.

Eventually our friend's eyes began to swim with tiredness and the book slipped from her grasp. Closing her eyes, she snuggled up to Indiana and slowly, something funbelievable began to happen. The sapphire in Indiana's collar and the matching stone in Aisha's necklace started to vibrate and pulse together as our heroes began to share exactly the same dream.

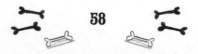

The face of the Avenger drifted into their thoughts. The knight looked happy and content. He was sitting in a red room, reading at a simple desk, stroking a small dog who was curled up asleep on his lap. In the dream the knight became aware that he had company. Smiling, he reached towards Indiana and rubbed his ears lovingly. Selecting a book from the shelves next to his desk, he held it out as if it was a gift. Aisha took the book, which turned to sand in her hands and slipped through her fingers. Then deep sleep finally swallowed them.

4

The Temple of Artemis

Aisha woke next morning bathed in delicious sunbeams that poured through Jovis's bedroom window. The little boy's top bunk was already empty and Aisha could hear the sound of a

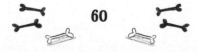

ball being kicked around outside. The glorious weather, combined with the book and the dream of the helpful, friendly knight, put Aisha in a much more positive frame of mind. Okay, the journal was gone, but she had already come within a wolf's whisker of the treasure without it, so maybe all was not lost. She decided that she would talk to her dad; maybe between them both they could pick up the treasure trail another way.

Aisha tickled one of Indiana's alarmpits. 'Wakey-wakey! Who's my pal? I'm done moping around with the Mayor of Mopetown on my mopey old moped – we need to get back on the hunt.'

'Mmm. Five more minutes,' grumbled Indiana, rolling over.

'No chance, thunderpants,' replied Aisha. 'We nearly struck gold without the journal. We can do it again.'

Indiana sat up with a glint in his eye. Being a dog in an archaeological family meant that he also had the bug. The dream had left him feeling strangely as though the knight was with them somehow. 'I had the strangest dream about the Lonely Avenger,' he said to his pal.

'Me too,' said Aisha. 'He was sitting in a red room and he gave us a . . .'

'Book?' said Indiana, finishing his friend's sentence.

'Yes,' said Aisha. 'Oh wow! Super spooky.'

'Do you think the book was a clue?' Indiana

asked. 'Maybe he wants us to use books to try and track him down.'

Aisha showed him the book she'd been reading the night before. The scruffy pooch felt a pang, wishing he could read as well as Aisha, but that thought was replaced by the most brilliant idea about where they should look next. 'Wait,' he exclaimed, rushing off to Julimus's bookshelves to gather books, pictures and maps.

As you know, Indiana was a magical dog and he was able to remember many words and simple phrases. He was good with maps and pictures, and he had taught himself to recognise and read easy words and sentences. But he was a dog who'd grown up in a home

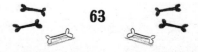

filled with books and ever since he was a little puppy, he'd ached to be able to read properly, *really properly*. He longed to devour entire books, in the way that Aisha and Dr Ghatak did, but when faced with a whole book, the shapes of the words shifted and swam around on the page and no matter how he tried he could not tame them.

But right now, he had an idea and he knew that together with Aisha, he could explain what he was thinking.

'Great!' said Aisha, when Indiana returned. 'Let's get Dad.'

They were delighted to find Dr Ghatak alone in the kitchen. Julimus had gone to the British Museum with the journal, and Celia seemed to

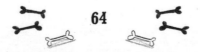

have slipped out yet again. Indiana plonked his stuff on the table.

'Dad,' began Aisha. 'I'm sorry about yesterday. I was disappointed about the journal, but I know you're right. The oldest book in the world deserves to be in a museum and it would have been terrible if it had crumbled and disintegrated in our hands. But I think you and I and Indiana can quickly get back on the trail of the Lonely Avenger if we all put our heads together. I did some thinking last night and Indiana has an idea about where we can start.'

'That's my girl, Aisha, and that's my dog,' said her dad, pulling them both in for a cuddle. 'I hate it when we fight. We must try not to.

It gets in the way of everything. It gets in the way of archaeology, and in the way of you both becoming friends with Celia. I know you'll like her when you get to know her. There is a lot more to her than meets the eye. Say you'll give her a chance?'

'I definitely will,' said Aisha, looking up. 'If you like her, she can't be all that bad.'

'She is indeed not all that bad,' smiled Dr Ghatak. 'Now, Indiana, tell me your thoughts.'

Indiana Bones began to flick through books and place them open on the table. He laid out maps and drawings of buildings, starting with the lighthouse and the pyramids.

'Okay,' said Dr Ghatak, 'give us a clue.'

Indiana was buzzing like a faulty fridge,

and although Aisha L.O.V.E.D. loved seeing her pal excited, he was taking too long. She wished he would cut to the chase.

Eventually Dr Ghatak pleaded, 'Just tell us!'

'Right,' said Indiana. 'Let's have a recap. The Avenger visited the pyramids. We know that for certain.' Bones pointed at a map. 'If he sailed from France, here, around the coast of Spain, then the most likely place for him to stop in Egypt would be here, in Alexandria.'

Aisha joined in, 'From an archaeological point of view, there are two interesting things in Alexandria. One is a library – no big deal.'

'No big deal?' said Dr Ghatak, raising an eyebrow. 'The Great Library of Alexandria was one of the largest and most significant

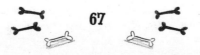

libraries of the ancient world. It was kind of a *massive deal.*'

'Okay,' said Aisha. 'What I mean is that the place we're really interested in is the lighthouse at Alexandria.'

'One of the Seven Wonders of the Ancient World,' said Dr Ghatak.

'Fizzactly,' said Indiana Bones. 'And where did he head next?'

'The pyramids,' said Aisha.

'Another of the Seven Wonders,' said Dr Ghatak.

'Confirmative!' said Indiana. 'So maybe the Avenger was heading around the world, visiting each of the Seven Wonders and stealing any treasure he could on the way . . . ?'

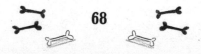

Dr Ghatak's eyes began to twinkle in that way they always did when something exciting was on the horizon. 'My goodness, you clever pair. I think you may be on to something! We know he visited the lighthouse and the Great Pyramid. It makes total sense that he would want to see the rest, especially if he was on the hunt for treasure.'

Aisha grinned too. 'So, the first thing we have to do is list the Seven Wonders.'

With the help of Julimus's books and maps, the three of them wrote a list and laid out pictures of the seven historic sites.

- Lighthouse at Alexandria
- Great Pyramid of Giza, Egypt

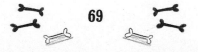

- Hanging Gardens of Babylon
- Statue of Zeus at Olympia
- Temple of Artemis at Ephesus
- Mausoleum at Halicarnassus
- Colossus of Rhodes

Indiana's brain whirred into action. 'The Avenger started at the lighthouse, then he went overland to the pyramids, which is where we found his journal. He must have gone back to Alexandria to pick up his boat – but where next? The Hanging Gardens of Babylon?'

Dr Ghatak thought for a moment. 'That's a tricky one. Historians know very little about the gardens and have long argued about where

they were. There is no evidence of them. No ruins, nothing.'

'Where is Babylon?' Aisha wondered.

'Central Iraq,' Dr Ghatak replied, showing her in the atlas.

'Well, I don't think he went there,' Aisha said.

'Why so sure?' her father asked.

'It's a VERY long way from the sea if he was trying to move treasure from the *Black Tiger*,' she replied. 'He might have visited, but I don't think it's where he would have stashed his loot.'

'Clever Aisha!' chimed Indiana. 'It's as though you know how the old knight was thinking!' He looked at the list again and asked, 'Where was the statue of Zeus?'

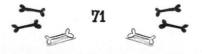

Dr Ghatak showed them Greece in the atlas. 'Here,' he said, pointing. 'He could have moored his ship on the coast and visited quite easily, but again it seems too far inland to transport a large quantity of treasure.'

'What's next?' said Indiana Bones. The archaeolo-dog was having a fine morning doing what he loved most with who he loved most.

'The Temple of Artemis at Ephesus,' said Aisha. 'Show me on the map.'

'Here.' Her father found Turkey. They all peered at it closely.

'Six miles from the coast, so unlikely but not impossible,' said Aisha. 'Hmm. We're not having much luck.'

'No, no, wait a second.' Dr Ghatak racked

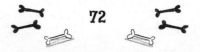

his brains. 'I've been to Ephesus many times, but it was a very different place two thousand years ago.'

He grabbed a Turkish travel guide from Julimus's shelves and flicked through to find a description of the city: 'Ephesus is an ancient Greek city on the west coast of Turkey. Fantastically well preserved, it has a grand theatre and a main street with arcades of shops which lead down to the Library of Celsus.'

Indiana sniffed at the picture of the library at Ephesus. 'Cool-looking building,' he said.

'But the most important thing is that it is the location of the Temple of Artemis,' said Aisha.

'Exactly,' smiled Dr Ghatak. 'Ephesus was once a great port, but it silted up over the

years, which is why the city is now inland. But in its heyday, I am pretty sure you could have sailed right into its centre.'

'Okay! So, we have a possibility,' said Aisha. She considered the knight's mission to plunder the world for treasure to build a shrine to his sweetheart. 'It is amazing what some people will do in the name of love,' she said, looking at her dad and wondering about Celia.

'My goodness!' her father whispered, suddenly turning pale and sitting down. '*In the name of love.* That's it! You've got it, Aisha. This *is* the place.'

'Do you mean Ephesus?' asked Indiana.

'Yes, more specifically the Temple of Artemis. I am sure of it.'

Aisha and Indiana looked at each other, then back at Dr Ghatak. 'Why?' she asked.

'It's all in the name,' replied Dr Ghatak. 'Artemis is a goddess in Greek mythology. She is one of the twelve Olympians – the daughter of Zeus and Leto, and sister of Apollo. She is the goddess of hunting, wild animals and the wilderness. But in Roman mythology – SHE IS KNOWN AS DIANA! And the French version of that name is Diane!'

Aisha gasped. The Lonely Avenger's one true love was called Diane!

'Where better for the Avenger to hide all the treasure stolen in the memory of his love than in a temple built for a goddess with the same name!' finished her father.

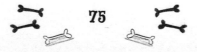

For a moment they were all speechless. This was H to the U to the G to the E to the H.U.G.E.

MASSIVE

Finally, everything was slotting into place. And Aisha was extra thrilled that her idea of working together had brought such quick results. Teamwork had helped them to climb inside the Avenger's mind and now they had a very strong sense of where his treasure might be.

Indiana Bones felt as pleased as Punch. 'We are ahead of the game now, Aisha,' he said. 'The Serpent and his fools have no idea about any of this. We may even have shaken them off at last.' He shared a grin with Aisha.

Their joy, however, was to be short-lived.

'I need to get a train to Turkey, and book a driver to take me to Ephesus. I shall call Charman and Dukes at once,' said Dr Ghatak.

'I'll pack my things!' said Aisha excitedly, but the look on her father's face stopped her.

Dr Ghatak shook his head. 'Not this time, my dear. It was tremendous of you to step in for me last time, but it's much safer for you to remain here.'

His words were sudden and unexpected. Aisha and Bones were stunned into silence.

'Don't worry though, if any treasure is found I will make sure you both receive full praise.' He smiled, as if his words made it all right. 'You can stay here and act as email and

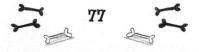

phone backup if I need any researchers. Now, where's my phone? I need to tell Edith I'm heading home to pack.'

Aisha and Indiana looked at each other. Full praise?

FULL.

PRAISE?

They were both acutely disappointed. Our heroes longed to be in the thick of things. But the way that Dr Ghatak had reacted about the journal the day before made them certain that there was no point in arguing. Sometimes it really sucked not to be a groan-up.

And that wasn't the only bad news, bookpals. On the other side of town, on the thirteenth floor of the building that looked

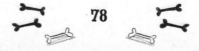

like a gherkin, things were stirring. When Dr Ghatak called Charman and Dukes, the Serpent's supercomputer clicked into action and two terrible words appeared in the corner of the monitor.

RECORD MODE

'Mr Charman, hello,' said Dr Ghatak into the receiver. 'It's Satnam Ghatak here ... I'm very well, thanks, and I hope you and Mr Dukes are too.'

Aisha and Indiana listened intently, and across town in the gherkin, the Serpent, Castle and Ringo listened too.

'I'm coming to see you, Mr Charman,'

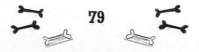

Dr Ghatak continued. 'I have some travel arrangements I would like your help with.'

'Yes, yes,' hissed the Serpent. 'We know that, but where are you thinking of going, Dr Ghatak?'

'I will explain everything tomorrow,' continued the archaeologist. 'Midday? Yes, perfect. See you then.'

The recording clicked off.

'Curses!' wheezed the Serpent. 'Clearly he is up to something. He knows exactly where to look next, but he gave nothing away! However, we do have some useful information. He *will* lead us to the treasure.'

Our vile villain typed at his keyboard and pulled up Julimus's address, tracked from the

phone line they had just hacked into. He gave it to Ringo.

'First, you and Mr Castle will go to Oxford to tail Ghatak. I will follow the action from here. Ringo, as soon as Dr Ghatak has been dealt with, you will get a fast train to London and keep an eye on the girl and her horrible hound, for they are dangerous and must not be allowed to become pests again. Quickly! Time is of the essence!'

He and Philip Castle began to make plans. Ringo listened as carefully as he could, determined not to muck anything up. Our smelly fool was very keen not to forget anything and so he scribbled himself a simple note on a scrap of paper:

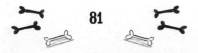

81

FinD out WHeRe
GHatak is Going

Locate TreasHure

~~Ele~~ ~~Elinim~~ ~~Itim~~
Eliminate GHatak

5

Oxford

The next morning, having stunk up the fast train from London the previous evening, Ringo awoke in a hotel on the outskirts of Oxford. You may think he could have stayed at Philip Castle's house, but unfortunately he was banned for life because Castle's cats were terribly allergic to his pong.

After opening his eyes, the big goon stretched twice and farted. I would like to tell you that he got up and showered before dressing, but that would be a lie, and as you know, friends don't lie. Instead, he clambered out of his bed and began putting on yesterday's clothes, which were also the day before yesterday's clothes.

Our slovenly slacker was so slothful, he'd decided against tying his shoelaces – after all, he would only have to undo them again at bedtime. Ringo didn't even go into the bathroom and wash his face, nor did he brush his Hula-Hoopy teeth. Instead, he scratched his bottom, ran his ring-infested fingers over his sweaty head, and set off, with the simple

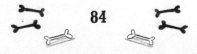

note of the plan not-very-carefully stuffed in his pocket.

Down in the hotel restaurant he ate one poached egg and drank two cups of coffee, before shuffling outside, where he smoked three disgustpig stinkarettes.

Although he had been given a job to do, Philip Castle and the Serpent didn't trust Ringo to do it alone, and so he was waiting to meet a couple of professionals who would help him complete his task without mucking it up.

His new accomplices arrived at nine forty-five and zero seconds, precisely on time. Their sleek black car with tinted windows pulled up silently and a rear door opened softly. Ringo

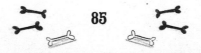

looked around proudly as if to say, 'Look at me, everybody, I'm going on a secret mission,' before squeezing his huge, scruffy frame awkwardly into the back of the car.

Ringo's new 'friends' looked identical to each other. They had been hired by the Serpent; their services secured overnight at great cost from an American contact. Both women were twenty-five point nine years old, 175 centimetres tall, and weighed seventy-six point seven kilos. Their short black hair was parted on the right and they wore matching black suits with black Aviator sunglasses. I, Sir Harold of Heape, am the writer of this book, and EVEN I don't have the right level of security clearance to be given their full names.

I only know them as Agent 1.0, who drove, and Agent 2.0, who sat alongside.

Ringo (Bonehead 3.1) settled himself in the back, not bothering to fasten his safety belt, and greeted his new colleagues with a friendly, 'Hello, ladies. I'm Ringo.' Disappointingly, the women felt no need to reply and the car sloped off silently towards the centre of Oxford. The women's nostrils soon began to twitch uneasily at the smell emanating from the back of the car. They both knew it was against mission protocol to travel on a job with the windows down. This, however, felt like paragraph 5.2, *Exceptional Circumstances*, and they simultaneously wound their windows down the regulation amount, to let in some fresh air.

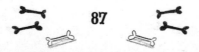

'We need to be quick,' said Ringo, feeling as though he was in charge. 'Time is of the essence.'

'Can it, Pongo,' said Agent 2.0. 'We are highly trained field operatives and aren't about to take any advice from a clown like you.'

Ringo drummed his fingers on the armrest as the car weaved smoothly in and out of traffic. Our smelly friend was starting to feel way out of his depth, like a Playmobil diver bobbing around in the Pacific Ocean. 'Why am I here?' he asked. 'You two look as though you can handle yourselves. Am I just along for the ride?'

'You are an integral part of the mission, sir,' smirked Agent 1.0, taking a corner like a

figure skater. This made Ringo feel a little bit better. Firstly, he was a *sir*; secondly, he was an important part of a mission; and thirdly, the woman's American accent made him feel as though he were in an exciting Hollywood film, like *Mission Improbable* or *Women in Black*.

'Excellent,' Ringo replied, raising an eyebrow, trying his best to look like James Bond.

Agent 2.0 explained further: 'You are important because if anything goes wrong, we need a big stupid dork to pin the blame on, while we sneak out the back door.'

The super-confident women laughed and high-fived each other, while Ringo's freshly found bubble of acceptance popped like a

bad burp at a barbecue. His heart sank, like unhappy fish poop, and he leaned back and tried to disappear into his seat.

Seven minutes later, the car pulled up outside the old-fashioned wood- and glass-fronted shop of Charman and Dukes, Oxford's oldest and most respected travel agents.

'Here's the plan,' said Agent 2.0, turning to Ringo. 'You go in to book a trip. Take up the old man's attention. Distract him. We'll sneak in, bug the place, and then, *pff*, we vanish into thin air.'

'What, just like that?' Ringo asked.

'Simple as,' replied 1.0.

'But what do I say?' Ringo wondered nervously.

'Act like you want a vacation, something fancy,' explained 2.0.

'C'mon, don't be a ninny-panted bum-hat,' added 1.0. 'Helicopter ride over Niagara Falls. Long weekend in Paris. A week in Rome. Athens. Anything. Use your brain and leave the rest to us.'

His brain? Ringo took a deep breath and stepped out of the car – and his comfort zone – and into Charman and Dukes. He strolled around, looking at brochures and pictures on the walls, trying very hard to seem normal. *I am not a ninny-panted bum-hat. I am not a ninny-panted bum-hat. I am not a ninny-panted bum-hat*, he repeated to himself, over and over, in his head.

Seconds later, Mr Charman joined him in front of the old wooden counter. 'May I help

you, sir?' he enquired politely, while thinking to himself, *What on earth is that frightful fug? Is this fellow part skunk?*

Nervous Ringo's mind went blank. 'I am not a ninny-panted bum-hat,' was the first thing that came out of his mouth.

'I'm sorry?' Mr Charman replied.

Ringo boggled at him. 'I mean ... Want holiday,' he said.

'Well, you've certainly come to the right place. Where exactly would Sir like to go?' Mr Charman asked politely, trying not to pass out from the awful stench now filling up his shop.

'Niagara Falls, Paris, Rome ... Athens,' replied Ringo, looking over his shoulder to see if 1.0 or 2.0 had slipped in yet.

'Are you expecting someone?' asked Mr Charman.

'Yes,' Ringo answered, quickly changing his mind to 'No.'

'So, do you want to go to Niagara, Paris, Rome, then Athens?' Mr Charman asked patiently.

'Yes,' replied Ringo. 'Then Blackpool,' he added, suddenly inspired.

'So, to be clear,' began Mr Charman, now dizzy with the pong. 'You wish to travel to Niagara Falls in Canada, then to Paris in France, then Rome in Italy and Athens in Greece, finally finishing in Blackpool, Lancashire.'

'Yes,' said Ringo, looking as pleased as a ~~pony with pigtails~~ pig with a ponytail.

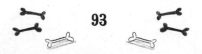

Mr Charman, beaten by the stench, found he could no longer concentrate. He excused himself for a moment to open a window at the back of the shop, and then slipped into the back office where he could get some air.

The second the elderly man had turned his back, Agents 1.0 and 2.0 appeared, as if by magic, from behind the counter.

'Gaah!' Ringo blurted in shock – he hadn't even seen them enter the shop. Within moments, like a well-oiled and choreographed machine, the slick Agent 1.0 jumped onto the shoulders of Agent 2.0 and attached a bug to the inside of the shade of the overhead light. Then she dropped noiselessly to the floor and the two of them slipped silently out of the shop door.

Wow, thought Ringo, for a moment frozen to the spot. Then, feeling like his job was also done, he scuttled out too, bumping into some shelving, knocking over a wastepaper basket and finally tripping over his untied shoelaces before exiting into the sunshine.

As he left, the simple, crumpled note he had written for himself fell out of his pocket and onto the polished mahogany floor.

When Mr Charman returned, he was extremely relieved to find his shop empty of the stinker, though sadly not empty of stench. 'Strange fellow,' he said to himself. 'Whiffy as a camel's sock.'

He took a can of air freshener from under the counter and liberally sprayed the whole shop several times. He had no idea that, as he walked around, he kicked Ringo's fallen note out of sight under the counter.

6

Number 33

Number 33 Avenue Lane in Oxford is the home of Dr Ghatak, his daughter Aisha and their magi-dog, Mr Indiana Bones. Those of you who have visited before will know that it is a large and beautiful Georgian town house overlooking communal gardens, with the spires of the

famous university kissing the clouds in the distance. The garden at the back slopes gently down to the River Thames, which wiggles slowly and gently, like well-educated treacle, through booky old Oxford towards somewhere called London.

Dr Ghatak and Celia arrived at the house in a cab they had caught outside the train station. Celia lifted out her luggage and waited while Dr Ghatak paid the driver.

'Are you really sure that you want to come all that way with me?' he asked, fishing in various pockets for his house keys. 'I am perfectly used to travelling on my own.'

'I know you are, Satnam, but as I explained earlier, I am meeting clients in Bulgaria who've

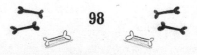

98

been burgled. I am helping them recover some of their *losses*,' said Celia. 'I don't think you were listening though; you had that far-off glint in your eye.'

'I'm sorry, of course you did,' said Dr Ghatak. 'It will be lovely to have your company on the journey. Bulgaria is en route and so we will have plenty of time for tea and chatting on the way.'

In the kitchen they found the Ghataks' friend and lodger, Edith Ellinor, who stood and folded the Minecraft magazine she had been reading, and went to greet them.

'Oh Edith, hello,' smiled Dr Ghatak. 'This is my friend, Celia. Can't stop long. Just going to grab a few things and my backpack. I'm off to

Turkey, and Celia is going to Bulgaria, so we need to visit Charman and Dukes.'

'Right away?' said Edith. 'You've only just arrived!'

'Yes, I'm afraid so,' Dr Ghatak answered.

Celia and Edith said hello and shook hands.

'Satnam, you are always as busy as a centipede in a shoe shop,' scolded Edith. 'Does it ever occur to you that you could stay in one place for longer than thirty seconds?'

'Pinky-promise I'll have a lovely long relax on the train, Edith,' Dr Ghatak retorted with a cheeky twinkle.

Edith gave him a clip around the ear with the rolled-up magazine. 'Don't try and play me like a banjo. That is not what I meant and

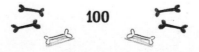

you know it,' she exclaimed. 'I've half a mind to send you to your room.'

Celia smiled. She liked Edith already.

'You worry too much,' said Dr Ghatak, emptying pockets of his wallet, keys and phone. He dropped them onto a table in the hall and rushed up the stairs two at a time to pack. 'Come on!' he shouted over his shoulder to Celia.

A matter of moments later, Dr Ghatak and Celia reappeared downstairs, weekend bags at the ready.

'That was speedy, even for you, Satnam,' said Edith, putting down her magazine on the hall table and adjusting her old friend's shirt collar. 'Off you go, then. Lovely to meet you, Celia.'

'By the way,' said Dr Ghatak, 'Aisha and Indiana are still in London, staying with Julimus. I shall collect them both on my return, and then maybe we can all relax together for a day or two.'

'I shall believe that when I see it,' said Edith.

Dr Ghatak picked up his keys and his wallet, and he and Celia stepped outside.

Satnam Ghatak had a real soft spot for delicious motor vehicles. Aisha and Indiana had borrowed his flame-red Ducati motorbike during their previous gladventure. For today's journey, he chose his powder-blue Mercedes 300, which he backed out of the garage at the side of 33 Avenue Lane. It was a two-seater

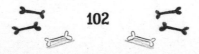

sports car without a roof, the kind of car you can only really drive on a sunny day (and also the kind of car that you *really want* to drive on a sunny day). Dr Ghatak put his backpack and Celia's luggage on the back seat, and pulled slowly out of the drive.

Sunglasses on and grey hair swept back in a ponytail, Dr Ghatak turned onto the main road and drove past a row of ramshackle shops towards Temple Cowley. He was in a very good mood. A delicious sense of possibility stretched out in front of him and he was feeling the start of this adventure so keenly he could almost reach out and rub its belly.

From Temple Cowley, the blue Mercedes took the scenic route along the road which

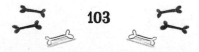

closely followed the Thames. The slick sports car hugged the tarmac and weaved alongside the meandering river, passing boaters enjoying the water and picnickers eating Monster Munch sandwiches on Christ Church Meadow. It wasn't long before they pulled up outside Charman and Dukes.

As Celia and Dr Ghatak entered the shop, they failed to notice a large, very sleek black surveillance van with tinted windows parked opposite. Inside it were two of the three members of this book's Bad Team. The Serpent, as was his way, was safely coiled in his futuristic London office space. He was, as you know, a man who liked to get others to do his dirty work whenever he could. So it

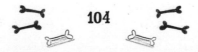

was just Ringo and Castle in the back of the van in Oxford city centre, sitting at a bank of computer monitors mounted above a sound desk. Both wore headphones connected to the bug inside the travel agency, and to the slithery Serpent inside the gherkin. All three of the Bad Team sat in anticipation, keen to hear the exact arrangements which they hoped were about to unfold inside the recently bugged shop.

Mr Charman beamed when he saw who his latest customers were. 'Good morning, Dr Ghatak,' he said. He looked at the eminent archaeologist and then at Celia, who he had not met before.

'Mr Charman, this is my good friend Celia Kane.'

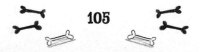

'Wonderful to meet you,' enthused old Mr Charman, shaking Celia's hand and making her feel most welcome. 'And how may we be of assistance today?'

Mr Charman offered his customers a seat on the tall stools next to the old mahogany counter. 'Might I suggest a weekend in a Norwegian ice hotel? A turtle-spotting holiday in the Galapagos Islands, perhaps? How about trekking through the jungle to Machu Picchu?'

'They all sound wonderful!' smiled Celia, who rather liked the idea of an exotic jaunt.

'I need to get to Turkey,' explained Dr Ghatak quietly, looking around to make sure the shop was as empty as a shlempty pempty. 'It needs to be rather hush-hush and under

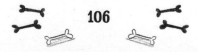

the radar. I am on the cusp of something sensational and splendid.'

'I understand,' replied Mr Charman. The old man walked slowly to the shop door, pulled the bolt across and turned the shop sign to 'Closed' so that they could not and would not be disturbed.

'Thank you,' said Dr Ghatak appreciatively as Mr Charman returned to his side of the counter.

'Now,' began the elderly gentleman, 'tell me exactly what you need.'

'I must get to Ephesus,' said Dr Ghatak. 'As you know, I prefer not to fly if possible. We'd like something a little more relaxed.'

'A gentle journey to Ephesus! Of course,'

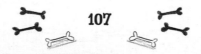

exclaimed Mr Charman. 'The world's finest surviving example of a Graeco-Roman classical city. A tantalisingly beautiful treat for two.'

'For one,' said Dr Ghatak. 'Although we are starting the journey together, Celia will only travel as far as Bulgaria. She will get off in Sofia.'

'I'm in insurance,' Celia explained, adjusting her hair. 'A client has lost something rather valuable and I need to meet her and offer my assistance.'

'Very good,' said Mr Charman. 'I think I have just the ticket. There is the most magnificent steam train that travels between Paris and Istanbul, calling at many beautiful cities. The last stop before Istanbul is Sofia.'

'Sounds perfect,' said Celia.

'You will travel through seven countries in elegant style,' Mr Charman continued. 'Food, wine, first-class service, fabulous ambience: everything is wonderfully over-the-top. Shall I book you one of the Grand Suites?'

'Please do,' replied Dr Ghatak. 'And how about the last part of the journey?'

'I shall call my dear old friend, Dr Emine Aziz,' said Mr Charman. 'She is a retired geologist, who keeps herself busy taxiing holidaymakers around Turkey. She will meet you at Istanbul station and deliver you to Ephesus in her jeep. I think you will like her very much.'

'That sounds splendid!' Dr Ghatak exclaimed.

'You'll arrive in Istanbul on Tuesday morning, and should reach Ephesus by late afternoon or early evening,' Mr Charman told him. 'I shall arrange lodgings for you in nearby Selçuk.'

'Your service, as always, is superb,' smiled Dr Ghatak.

'*Superb indeed,*' hissed the Serpent into Ringo's and Castle's headphones. '*We shall intercept Ghatak's driver with one of our own. He can lead us directly to where he believes the treasure to be located and then . . .*' he grinned a slithery grin, '*. . . we shall have him locked up somewhere revolting.*'

Thanking Mr Charman for his help, Dr Ghatak and Celia went off for a spot of lunch

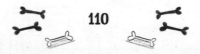

while arrangements were made. They were to return for the tickets in an hour. Mr Charman called Mr Dukes, who arrived excited to see Dr Ghatak. The elderly gentlemen of travel had often helped their favourite customer, if he was in a rush, by looking after whichever fantastic vehicle he had arrived in. And so, with big grins on their faces, Mr Charman and Mr Dukes agreed to drive Dr Ghatak's powder-blue Mercedes back to his house. It was something they had done many times before, and greatly enjoyed. They would take a longer, more scenic route to Avenue Lane and play loud opera on the car's stereo, while the whizzing of the wind whipped their white hair around their happy faces.

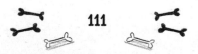

Celia and Dr Ghatak crossed the road directly in front of the surveillance van, oblivious of it and its malevolent inhabitants. Inside Castle grinned. 'Gotcha, Ghatak.'

The bugging of Charman and Dukes had been a great success. Our baddies knew Dr Ghatak was travelling to Turkey for the Avenger's treasure, they knew how he was getting there and who he was travelling with. For once, my friends, they were ahead of the game.

Castle turned to Ringo. 'You've had your orders. Now go and keep an eye on the girl and the dog. We'll look after Ghatak, but the last thing we need is that child turning up with her dumb mutt and messing up our plans again.'

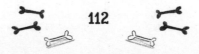

The Serpent too whispered a warning to Ringo through his headphones, his voice dripping with menace. 'Make sure they don't see you. And clean yourself up. The dog will be able to smell you from twenty miles away. Understand?'

'Yes, sir,' replied Ringo, shaking. 'I won't let you down.'

7

Full Steam Ahead

After picking up the tickets from Mr Charman, Dr Ghatak and Celia returned to London and stayed the night at Julimus's apartment. Now they were rushing around, checking that they had everything they needed before catching the early train from St Pancras to Paris, where they would meet the steam train that would take them all the way across Europe to Bulgaria and Istanbul.

Aisha was trying to put on a brave face, but it wasn't working. It was bad enough being left behind, but now she had to share her dad with someone else — someone she wasn't sure she could trust — it made her feel twice as bad. Indiana's sixth sense told him that Celia was hiding something and they both wondered what she might be up to. Could she be in league with Lupton? It was odd that she'd disappeared at the mention of the Serpent's name. Now Celia was going on a steam train to Istanbul on a treasure hunt that really felt like it was Aisha and

Indiana's adventure. Hadn't our heroes been the ones to find the Avenger's scroll? Hadn't they tracked the long-dead French knight all the way to Egypt and right into the belly of a pyramid where they'd found his journal and his sword? Yes, they honking well had! So why should they be the ones staying at home, kicking around the house like chilly cats in cashmere cardigans?

'Goodbye, my love,' said Dr Ghatak to Aisha, pulling her in for a cuddle. Aisha fought against the angry tears welling up inside her. 'I won't be away too long. I know everything feels new and strange and that you wish you could come too, but it's too dangerous. My number one job in the world

is to look after you. It's better that you stay here and take care of Indiana. I will see you soon.'

Celia smiled at Aisha, as if she understood how rubbish our hero was feeling, and with that they were gone.

Aisha looked at Julimus, who, after all they had been through together in Egypt, understood and shared her frustration. Trying to hide her tears, she sat down with Indiana. He snuffled Aisha lovingly with his cold nose. 'Who's my pal?' he asked, which at least made Aisha think about doing the tiniest little smile.

Julimus looked down at them. 'Cheer up, my friends! I have an exciting secret plan,' he said tantalisingly. 'If it works, you, I and

Indiana will be able to jump right back into this adventure without even leaving London.'

Aisha perked up. 'Tell me!'

'I will when I have everything in place,' he replied. 'This idea may enable you to help your father more than you can possibly imagine!'

And then he too was gone, leaving Indiana, Aisha and Jovis alone in the quiet apartment.

'What did Julimus mean?' said Aisha.

'I don't know. He talks in riddles,' replied Indiana.

'He is very good at mending problems,' said Jovis. 'Maybe he will help mend this one.'

'Maybe he's going to bring the journal back for us to read,' said Aisha hopefully.

'No chance,' said Indiana. 'He promised Dr

Ghatak he wouldn't. Besides, it probably would actually turn to dust, and none of us wants that to happen.'

'So how can he possibly help?' said Aisha, going around in circles. Indiana did not have an answer for his friend.

'You'll just have to wait and see,' said Jovis, looking like a pint-sized version of his father, a hopeful twinkle in his eye.

After turning things over a hundred times and getting nowhere, Aisha felt frustration get the better of her, so they all went out onto the rooftop to kick a ball around. This turned out to be a reasonable distraction. They spent a happy couple of hours, taking it in turns to go in goal.

As they played, they were totally unaware

that they were being watched. A strange woman with blonde hair and thick dark sunglasses was observing their game from a neighbouring upstairs window. She could not take her eyes off them.

When the sun started to dip below the horizon and it grew colder, Aisha realised that she felt as hungry as a caterpillar. They retreated indoors and reheated some of the leftover puttanesca. Aisha didn't want to admit it, but it tasted even better this time.

They were all happy, full and relaxed with contented tummies when they were interrupted by Aisha's phone ringing. To her surprise, she saw the call was from Edith. 'Hello,' she answered. 'You okay, Edith?'

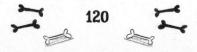

'Yes, my love. But listen. I've had a rather worrying call from Mr Charman. It seems that some vagabond was in the shop earlier, who he said did not smell so good.'

Aisha sat bolt upright. 'Ringo!' she said to Indiana, who also now moved into super-alert mode. 'What happened, Edith?'

'Mr Charman said the man was acting oddly,' continued the woman. 'But he didn't think anything of it until he found a crumpled-up note under the counter. It mentions your father.'

'I'll ring him,' said Aisha. 'Call you back in a second, Edith.'

Aisha hung up and rang her dad's number.

Ring ring. Ring ring. Ring ring. Ring ring.

'Pick up, Dad,' Aisha pleaded into her phone. 'PICK UP!' but still the phone just rang. 'Come on, come on.'

She was about to give up when suddenly the phone was answered. 'Dad?'

'No. It's me again, Edith. Your foolish father has left his phone on the table in the hall.'

'Oh dear,' replied Aisha. 'What did the note say, Edith? Did Mr Charman tell you?'

'Yes,' replied Edith. 'It said: *FIND OUT WHERE GHATAK IS GOING, LOCATE TREASURE* and *ELIMINATE GHATAK*.'

Aisha gulped. 'Thank you, Edith. I'll find a way to get a message to my father.' And with that she hung up.

Turning to Indiana Bones, she said, 'Dad's in

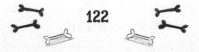

trouble. Somehow the Serpent and his cronies have found out his plans and they're after him. He left his phone at home, so we can't warn him. What on earth are we going to do?'

Indiana looked at his pal. This was serious.

'There's only one thing we can do,' said Indiana. 'We get the next train to Paris, and then to Turkey. We have to hope that we can get to your father before the Serpent does.'

8

Things Begin to Really Hot Up

This next section of the book is very juicy, my lovely book gobblers, the adventure starts to really cook, and as a result, there is plenty for you to chew on. Things begin to really hot up, so I have decided to call this chapter 'Things Begin to Really Hot Up'.

For Aisha Ghatak and Indiana Bones, time was as tight as the skinny jeans of a teenage T-Rex. As soon as they had made up their mind to follow Dr Ghatak and Celia to Turkey, whoosh, they were on their way. Satnam and Celia had left that morning. If our heroes could make one of the afternoon trains to Paris, they'd be less than a day behind them, which didn't feel too bad.

Aisha had hurriedly thrown everything she thought they might need into her backpack. With Charman and Dukes' help, she quickly researched the journey they would be making to Turkey and, not wanting Julimus to worry,

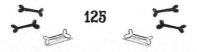

she hastily scribbled a note to let him know about Ringo and to fill him in on their plans.

'Here,' said Aisha to Jovis, pressing the note into his hands. 'Give this to your dad.'

'It's a shame you can't travel with us,' said Indiana to the boy. 'Last time you were awesome and found the Avenger's journal. And I shall definitely miss your excellent cuddling,' he added, nuzzling in to say 'goodbye'.

'Tell your dad we'll be in touch as soon as we can,' Aisha said, as Indiana pulled out from his long goodbye snuggle.

They left Julimus's apartment and crossed the busy road. As they walked, they did not notice the strange woman with the blonde hair who'd been spying on them earlier. She followed

at a safe distance, and while Indiana glimpsed her at one point, he thought nothing of it. He and Aisha were focusing only on getting to St Pancras train station as quickly as possible.

When they arrived, Aisha and Indiana bought their tickets and boarded the sleek Eurostar that would take them on the first leg of their journey. As always, there was a small kerfuffle when Indiana Bones showed his pet passport. Aisha loved to tease him about his photo. It had been taken when his hair was in a particularly long phase and so he looked very much like a poodle, with his eyes hidden somewhere behind a shaggy curtain of curls. 'You could be wearing sunglasses behind all that hair and no one would know,' she joked.

Aisha and Indiana took their places in a quiet carriage. The train was practically empty and they were able to sit well away from any other passengers. This was good. It meant they would be able to talk to each other without fear of being overheard. The last thing they needed was to arrive in Paris having gone viral because some random traveller had posted a video of the only talking dog in the whole world.

Behind them, the mysterious blonde lady that Indiana had glimpsed earlier, but thought nothing of, boarded the train two carriages along. He saw her again now, and thought nothing of it once more.

The train out of London was quick and

quiet. Before you could say, 'They'd left the city behind them,' they'd left the city behind them. Everything felt exciting as a sandwich as our heroes whizzed through the Kent countryside towards the coast.

Aisha was a self-assured traveller, but she was worried about how her dad would fare when he got to Turkey. She hoped they would be able to catch up with him in time and regretted deeply that they had quarrelled so fiercely about the journal.

Time passed as quickly as a shmickley pickley and they soon arrived at Folkestone, and then the Channel Tunnel. The tunnel was a fantastic feat of engineering. Aisha knew it ran seventy-five metres under the seabed,

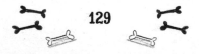

which was a huge heap of digging, and the young archaeologist felt glad she'd not had to help with her trowel. This part of the trip would take thirty-five minutes, and then, as if by magic, they would pop out in France. The English sky disappeared behind them and they entered the brightly lit tunnel with its orange fluorescent glow.

Aisha closed her eyes, suddenly tired, and fell into a fitful forty winks. She dreamed of knights and treasure and of trying to find her father, who was in turn looking for Celia.

She awoke with a jolt to find herself most definitely in France. Wriggling in her seat, she looked out of the window and thought about how everything seems different when you are

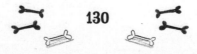

abroad – the red-roofed houses, the way people dressed, the exotic road signs. Aisha loved this feeling. She was thrilled to be in Europe, and whispered a quiet *bonjour* to a seagull sitting on a French chimney pot.

Blinking hard, trying to wake up properly, Aisha took a sip of water from the bottle in her backpack. She stroked Indiana and relaxed, glad that they were on an adventure again. With good planning and a bit of luck, they would find Dr Ghatak and all would be well.

She was almost on the verge of nodding off again when a ping from her phone brought her fully awake. Pulling it out, she was immediately excited.

'Indiana!' she whispered. 'It's from Julimus.'
The two pals huddled together and Aisha read the email quietly to Indiana.

Dear Aisha and Indiana,

Hello there! I trust that you are both well. Thank you for keeping me abreast of your travel plans. Forgive me for disappearing so quickly and not telling you what I was up to. I had been placed in a tricky position by Dr Ghatak. I promised your father that I would not let you get your hands on the Avenger's journal because it was so fragile – your father was completely right!

'Completely wrong, more like,' grumbled Aisha.

'Keep reading,' Indiana urged, wishing very much he could just read it himself. 'What else does he say?'

Aisha looked back at her phone.

But I also knew how important it was to find out what was written in the journal. At the British Museum, we have an X-ray machine which helps us to look at very fragile artefacts. I have placed the journal inside this wonderful machine, which allows me to examine each page in turn for clues without even touching the book. If there is anything at all useful inside the journal, I should be able to send you the

information. It is early in my investigation, but I can tell you that the Lonely Avenger spent some time in Alexandria.

'As we guessed!' said Aisha.

'Confirmative,' nodded Indiana.

It appears he had a travelling companion when he arrived in Alexandria, a puppy called Amie.

'Cute!' said Aisha. '*Amie* is French for "friend". Why do I feel like I love this knight?'

Indiana too liked this idea of the knight's dog very much and the sapphire in his collar agreed, pulsing strongly and changing to a

deep slatey blue, like the colour of the sea around Skara Brae.

Aisha continued,

Our knight went there initially to look at the lighthouse, but it seems that he became obsessed with the Great Library. I have attached a picture of the library from my first X-ray of the journal.

'Yay, I love pictures,' enthused Indiana. 'Let's see it.'

Aisha clicked on the attachment and an illustration of a magnificent building opened on the screen.

'Wowzers,' said Aisha and Indiana together.

There was something mesmerising about this building coming to life before their eyes. Had it been drawn by the knight himself? Or had a travelling artist drawn it for him? Either way, it felt like pure magic. Here they were, on a train speeding through France, discovering the secrets of a long-dead knight that had come alive in an emailed X-ray!

'What else? What else? What else?' asked Indiana.

Aisha quickly read the rest of the message. 'That's pretty much it,' she said. 'Julimus says he'll email again when he's done more scans.'

'This is good,' whispered Indiana. 'Who knows what he'll find! I wonder if the Avenger

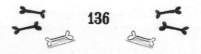

wrote down any cool Egyptian recipes. I want to learn how to make kushari.'

'Who's my pal, you big foodle-poodle!' said Aisha. 'I was thinking more about whether he would lead us straight to the treasure.'

'Er, yes, of course,' blushed Indiana. 'The more treasurey-information we can find out from that journal, the better.'

While Aisha replied to Julimus, Indiana counted pylons flying past outside the window and dreamed about North African cuisine. They were so engrossed, neither of them noticed the mysterious blonde lady who'd now come to sit at the other end of their carriage. Whoever she was, she was getting braver. And more worryingly, she was getting closer.

9

Chess

Apart from four cups of tea, eight aloo parathas, three Babybels, nine fizzy peaches, a Curly Wurly and the world's longest game of I-spy, the rest of the journey was uneventful. The Eurostar was now gliding through the outskirts of Paris. France's capital city was finishing work for the day and wondering what it could possibly have for supper.

Aisha and Indiana rested their chins on their folded arms and gazed out at the Parisian suburbs. On train journeys, Aisha usually loved to try to catch little glimpses of ordinary people going about their lives in back gardens and in municipal parks. Outside, rainclouds were beginning to gather over the French capital. Aisha hoped that this was not an omen for the rest of their journey.

Aisha saw block after block of flats and glass-fronted office buildings. She glimpsed bridges and warehouses covered in thick, colourful French graffiti. And just for an exciting moment, in the distance, silhouetted

against the grey sky, she spotted the famous Eiffel Tower.

The buildings became much closer together, more densely packed, as they entered the heart of the city and started passing slowly through tunnels and under bridges. Aisha knew that they were approaching Paris's main rail station, the grand Gare du Nord.

Unfortunately, the Istanbul train did not leave until the following morning and so they had acres of time to kill. They ate at a cafe before curling up together and catching snatches of broken sleep in one of the station's many waiting rooms.

When they woke up next day, everywhere bustled busily. There was a hurly-burly of

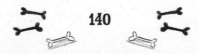

travellers pulling suitcases behind them. Young, old, children, grandparents, backpackers and a great many smartly dressed French none-of-your-business men.

Aisha and Indiana made their way to the ticket office and bought two singles to Istanbul. Luckily, it wasn't long before their train was due to depart. There was just time to pick up a couple of sandwiches – cheese for Aisha and tuna for Indiana – and then to indulge in one of Aisha's favourite travel treats. They sneaked into one of the French perfume shops lining the Gare du Nord's busy arcade, where Aisha gave herself a generous squirt of expensive perfume, and Indiana Bones had a lovely blast of even more expensive aftershave.

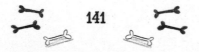

'Thanks,' whispered Indiana. 'I feel like Captain America now.'

'Scooby-Doo, more like,' laughed Aisha, and tickled one of his doggy alarmpits. Finally, with a spring in their step, and smelling all nice, they rode the escalator down to the platform where the Istanbul Express was waiting, it seemed, just for them.

This modern-looking train was as sleek as a bullet and much busier than Aisha had expected. It would be quicker than Dr Ghatak's train and Aisha hoped they would be able to catch her father up before their enemies could get to him. There would, however, be no quiet carriage for them on this leg of the journey, which meant our travelling companions

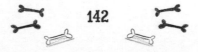

would have to keep their chitter-chatter to themselves.

Theirs was the last carriage of the long train. Making their way to the end of the platform, they climbed aboard and quickly found their seats. Unbeknown to our heroes, the mysterious blonde woman was still hot on their trail. Hiding under a large sun umbrella, she walked along the platform, just outside their window, and took her seat in the next carriage.

Aisha stuffed her backpack into the luggage holder above their seats and they settled down next to each other. Indiana immediately curled up and closed his eyes. 'You can't seriously be going to sleep already!' whispered Aisha.

'You've only just woken up!' She gave him a grumpy prod.

Indiana returned her look guiltily, as if to say, maybe just the smallest of sneaky snoozes? Aisha smiled a smile, which her beloved dog knew meant, *Oh, go on then, you big hairy goofball, snooze away.*

To keep herself amused, Aisha looked at a book she'd downloaded onto her phone. It was the one she had started at Julimus's house: *Alexandria to the Pyramids, an Archaeological Journey.* Reading to herself, she stroked Indiana's big floppy ears. 'You've got the right idea,' she whispered. It was a long journey to Istanbul and Aisha knew full well that Indiana would spend most of it dreaming of

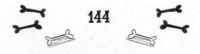

being the manager of the world's biggest dog biscuit factory.

Their first stop was in Stuttgart in Germany that afternoon. Here they were joined at their table by a stern-looking gentleman, who placed his luxurious luggage in the rack up above them.

His hair was short, as black as midnight, and receding ever so slightly. He had the most striking and intense green eyes either side of an elegant nose. He was dressed in a smart black suit and tie, and pointed black leather ankle boots which shone as if they had been polished only moments before. In short, he looked immaculate. He carried with him an umbrella, even though it hadn't rained in weeks, and a black leather document case.

Aisha smiled a hello, but her friendliness was ignored. The man furrowed his brow as he sat down opposite. Aisha was sure that he tutted quietly when he looked at Indiana.

Aisha continued to read, occasionally sneaking glances at the man. She noticed a brass plate on his document case that read *Dimitar Vakondember*, and assumed that this was his name.

Aisha spent much of that day reading and doing word searches, while Indiana either slept or looked out of the window at the world whizzing by.

Eventually, she finished her book and began to get as wriggly as a restless rattlesnake, which annoyed the frowny Mr Vakondember.

So, it was much to Aisha's surprise when he suddenly spoke to her.

'Chess?'

'I beg your pardon?' she replied. His question, after they had been sitting together for hours and hours, came somewhat out of the blue.

'Would you like a game of chess?' he repeated.

'Err, sure,' replied Aisha, who had played a million games with her dad on journeys just like these.

Mr Vakondember opened his document case and pulled out an antique chess set. The board was set into the lid of a shallow cylindrical box. Mr Vakondember twisted the lid, which

came off and revealed the pieces inside, each one in its own special compartment, lined with velvet.

'Nice set,' Aisha remarked, thinking how much her dad would like it. 'Persian?'

'Very good,' replied Mr Vakondember. 'Specialist knowledge for a young lady.' There was something about the way that he said this that made Aisha feel as though he was interrogating her. 'What are you so engrossed in with on your telephone? Is it Candy Crush?'

'No,' replied Aisha, slightly annoyed. 'I've been reading *Alexandria to the Pyramids, an Archaeological Journey.*'

Mr Vakondember nodded. 'Ambitious,'

he said. His searching green eyes seemed to suggest that Aisha was breaking some unwritten law about what children were and weren't allowed to read.

As Mr Vakondember arranged the chess pieces for a game, Aisha decided to set him straight. 'It's because I am an archaeologist,' she told him.

'I detest archaeologists,' said Mr Vakondember coolly. 'You are still young and should most certainly consider an alternative career. Archaeologists are little more than common thieves.'

Good grief, this man was mean and rude! Aisha was not at all sure she liked him. 'Not all of them,' she replied.

'Yes. All of them. All of them that I have ever met, or indeed heard of, apart from one notable exception,' Mr Vakondember declared.

Oh great, Aisha thought to herself. *What a barrel of laughs. I wish he'd just kept quiet. I shall enjoy completely destroying him at chess.*

She rolled up her sleeves and narrowed her eyes. The two settled down to playing, moving their pieces cagily. Both were proud and wanted to defeat each other, and it turned out they were evenly matched.

Indiana Bones was not interested in chess. As Aisha and the man began their battle, he looked down the aisle of the train carriage. The doors at the far end opened and the mysterious blonde woman entered. As before,

Indiana would not have paid her much mind, but she was right in his line of vision as she came through the carriage. The first thing he noticed was that she was wearing dark sunglasses and gloves, even inside the train. And she had an unusual, lolloping walk, like a cartoon character.

As she passed, Indiana began to growl quietly. 'Shh, grumpy old goose,' said Aisha, giving him a friendly rub.

Indiana observed the blonde lady as she moved through the train, and things began to stir in his brain. He felt as though he had seen her before – yes, he had! On the street near Julimus's apartment, and at St Pancras station! And maybe it wasn't just a coincidence.

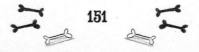

He watched her make her way through their carriage. Was she looking for a toilet? Indiana wondered. As theirs was the last carriage, she had nowhere left to go and, realising that, she turned and walked back, right past our hairy hero. The two of them locked eyes for a moment as she moved back the way she had come. Needing a stretch, Indiana decided to follow her at a distance, through their carriage and the next one too. He watched as she eventually found a toilet and slipped inside. Indiana walked past and hid just around the corner, where he waited and waited. This was as odd as a sock. She was taking a long time. What could she be doing in there for so long?

Eventually the woman came out, scratched

at her blonde hair and headed back to her seat. Indiana slipped into the small room she had vacated. The air was thick with the smell of cheap perfume. Indiana coughed and opened the tiny window so he could breathe properly, then sniffed around. Were the smells he was picking up under the perfume familiar? Almost, he thought.

Feeling curious and intrigued, Indiana Bones headed back to his own seat.

Aisha and Dimitar Vakondember were still engrossed in the most epic of contests. They felt as though they were involved not just in a chess battle, but in a war of personalities and will.

'So why don't you like archaeologists?' Aisha asked him.

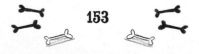

'I work for the Bureau of Missing International Artefacts,' the man replied. 'Most missing artefacts around the world have been taken illegally by archaeologists. They are, in short, the enemy of the bureau.'

'Archaeologists have a duty to give what they find back to the people,' said Aisha, taking one of Mr Vakondember's pawns. 'And most do,' she added.

'Debatable,' replied her opponent, taking one of Aisha's pawns. 'Anyway, my job is just a way to finance my real passion. My enthusiasms lie ... elsewhere.' He studied the chessboard like a general would a battlefield.

'Oh really,' replied Aisha, reminding herself to say as little as possible about the nature of

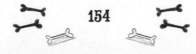

her journey. 'And what is that?'

'I am an inventor,' he told her. 'Though not a very successful one,' he added, with something which could almost be described as the beginnings of a smile. 'You would love my latest invention. I call her Old Meg.'

Aisha liked inventors – at least, the ones that she had read about in books. She would have liked to hear more about Old Meg, though she thought it would probably turn out to be something disappointing, like a self-folding camping table or an automatic cat feeder.

Unfortunately, Mr Vakondember had returned to talking about his day job. 'The vast majority of so-called archaeologists are simply common thieves with trowels,' he said

pompously. 'The priceless artefacts they steal then pop up in a museum far away from where they belong. Or worse – they vanish into the collections of wealthy individuals.'

Aisha did not like what this man was saying. What he said was partly true, but no way did it tell the whole story. However, she was in no mood to argue and tried instead to concentrate on winning the game. Common thieves? The cheek! She wanted to wipe the smile off his face, if only for a moment.

Indiana settled back into his seat, resting his chin on Aisha's lap. He longed to talk to her, but he couldn't while Mr Vakondember was there. For now, he would snooze and try to gather his thoughts. There was something

about the lady he'd followed which he wasn't happy about, and he could feel the sapphire in his collar pulsing gently.

Half an hour later, Aisha sat up straight in her seat. 'Checkmate!' she said, far more casually than she was actually feeling. On the inside she was dancing down the carriage and high-fiving other passengers at her victory over this pompous man. However, on the surface she kept her cool.

Mr Vakondember nodded in approval. 'I should very much like to play you again one day, young lady. You are a formidable opponent.'

He was so gracious in defeat that Aisha felt slightly warmer towards him. 'Thank you,

Mr Vakondember. I'm sure I was very lucky,' she lied.

'You played with skill,' he said, handing her one of his business cards.

Aisha and Indiana had both dozed off again when they were awoken by a loud gasp from Mr Vakondember. They opened their eyes to find him looking out of the window. 'Goodness,' he exclaimed. 'Budapest! My stop.' He gathered his things quickly. 'Goodbye, my young friend. I hope we meet again one day.' And then he was gone – out of the carriage, onto the platform, where he disappeared into the crowds.

Indiana yawned and looked about the carriage. He wanted very much to talk to Aisha about the strange lady, but the surrounding

seats were rapidly filling up with people joining the train in Budapest. He would have to continue the pretence of being a normal pooch for a while longer. Little did he know that by nightfall, events would have taken a turn for the worse and their plans of meeting Dr Ghatak in Turkey would be completely smashed to smithereens.

10

A True Friend in Times of Sorrow

It was early evening outside and it was already dark, which was good because it now felt as though time was actually passing. By morning they would be in Bulgaria and by the following afternoon, Istanbul in Turkey. From there Aisha thought they'd take a taxi to Ephesus, so in theory, by this time tomorrow, she would be reunited with her dad.

Aisha had never been to Istanbul before, but had heard all about it from her father, who *loved* the place. One of the things that fascinated Dr Ghatak was that Istanbul spanned two continents: half the city is in Europe and the other half is in Asia. And he had told her of course about Istanbul's history, how it had been known as Byzantium and then Constantinople, and was the jewel in the crown of the Ottoman empire.

'Istanbul,' Dr Ghatak had explained, 'is packed with most glorious reminders of

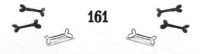

its long and illustrious history: the Hagia Sophia, Topkapi Palace, Blue Mosque and Grand Bazaar!' Aisha hoped that once they had rescued her father, they could stay a few days longer to look at all these exotic historical sites.

Just then, there was a ping from her phone and she was thrilled to see that it was another email from Julimus. There were too many people nearby for her to share it with Indiana, so she read it to herself, imagining Julimus's warm, gentle voice.

Dearest Ms Aisha Ghatak & Dearest Mr Indiana Bones,

How Jovis and I miss having you

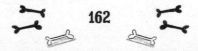

around the place! We hope that you are doing well. I imagine that you are both somewhere in south-eastern Europe, Hungary or even Bulgaria by now, heading speedily towards your father. I wish you both the very best of luck. If anyone can snatch him from the clutches of those rogues, then it is you two, my good friends.

I am sure that you will be interested to hear what I have managed to find from my latest scans of the journal and so I will move swiftly on.

What I have found is a wonderful story, Aisha, and like so many of the things we have learned about this knight, it is sad

but magnificent! One day, when this book comes to the attention of the public, it will be considered one of the most fantastic archaeological finds of all time. There will be films made about this knight of ours, I am sure of it!

Aisha's mind boggled and excitedly she read on.

As you remember from my earlier email, the Avenger arrived in Alexandria with his travelling companion, Amie, the dog. They quickly found the Great Library of Alexandria. There is a lovely description which took me most of yesterday to decipher. He called this place *A true friend*

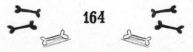

in times of sorrow, which, I am sure you will agree, seems like the perfect way to describe a library!

Then tragedy struck. The pair became separated in the crowds. The Lonely Avenger spent days looking for his Amie, but with no luck. He could only think that perhaps the dog had somehow ended up on one of the merchant boats in the harbour, destined for northern Europe. The knight was sad and he felt desperately unlucky. First he'd lost his true love, Diane, and now he'd lost his best friend, Amie.

Aisha fought back the tears that filled her eyes. She stroked Indiana's snoozing head in

her lap, unable to imagine being separated from her pal. The idea of it made her heart heavy and so she returned quickly to Julimus's email.

As a way to take his mind off Diane and Amie, the Avenger immersed himself in the world of the Great Library. Make no mistake, Aisha, this was the most exciting of times – the birth of books! For the first time in human history, people were writing and reading. It makes my spine tingle to hear about it from someone who was there. Our knight was happy beyond belief. He was due to stay just a week in Alexandria, but it seems romance was

calling. He clearly says in the journal that he fell in love for a second time.

Aisha felt shocked at this. Surely Diane was the knight's one and only true love?

I daresay you are surprised to read this, my dear. And so was I. But as the journal reveals a little further on, the knight had fallen in love not with another woman, but with books, reading and learning!

He had meant to stay just a week in Alexandria, but he ended up staying for months. He thought the library was the most perfect place in the world.

Books, he wrote, helped him with

the pain of losing Diana and Amie. He therefore planned to stay and read in Alexandria for the rest of his days. 'What could be better?' he wrote.

I have another section of pages to study this evening and I will email when I have more of the story to tell. Until then, stay safe my friends!

Best wishes,

Julimus

PS Jovis sends seven snuggles and five forehead kisses to Indiana.

Aisha's face broke into a big smile. It was great to hear from Julimus and even more exciting to

hear the words of her French knight, the Lonely Avenger. Even though he had lived more than two thousand years ago, he seemed very alive to Aisha. It was easy to imagine him strolling through the marketplace to that great library in Alexandria.

Putting her phone back in her pocket she gazed out of the train window at the twinkly lights whizzing by and her eyes began to close. Travel has a way of making you super tired and the carriage was now full of snoozers. As our hero's eyes closed, the third-eye sapphire in her necklace began to gently glow.

Indiana Bones, for a change, was merely pretending to sleep. He was thinking about the mysterious blonde woman. At Budapest,

with the change of passengers, Indiana had been concerned to see the woman move from the next carriage into the far end of this one. Now she'd caught his attention, it was pretty obvious she was following them. She was sitting with her back to our heroes, but from time to time she would turn to look up the carriage at them. It was very unsettling.

After hours of keeping a watchful eye, Indiana was dog-tired. He could fight it no more and decided to allow himself a mini nap.

Something woke our sleeping hero an hour later. It was quiet. Too quiet. The train was no longer moving and the carriage was in darkness. He popped his head up. How long

had they been stationary? Aisha slept on, but some of the other passengers were stirring and wondering what could be going on.

Indiana Bones looked down the train at the blonde woman and the moonlight illuminated her hair above the seat.

He decided to take a little walk to see if he could find out why they'd stopped. And this strange, quiet darkness seemed like a good time to let this woman know he was on to her, that he was watching, and to put her off any ideas she might have. Our favourite pooch stood and stretched, then made his way stealthily towards the other end of the carriage.

Placing paw after silent paw, he crept along the aisle. As Indiana Bones approached his

prey from behind, she was very still, obviously asleep. Even better! Chuckling to himself, Indiana decided he would make her jump out of her skin. However, as the shaggy dog peered around the seat, it was he who got a fright. It wasn't a person sitting there at all — it was a blonde wig, balanced on top of a rucksack. The woman was gone!

Indiana put two feet up on the chair and sniffed at the wig, taking in its scent. There was the cheap perfume again, and something stronger ... and very familiar!

Suddenly, there was a grating, twisting sound, followed by the noise of the train starting up again. And yet — this carriage remained still and in darkness.

In that moment, the penny dropped and Indiana knew exactly what was happening. He raced, rocket-like, towards the doors at the end of the carriage and pulled them open.

He was greeted by the sight of the rest of the train moving away, and the lady was standing at the back of it waving goodbye. Except it wasn't a lady – it was Ringo in a dress! He'd left the blonde wig behind. Gloves now removed, his ring-infested fingers had uncoupled the last carriage from the train and the front part was gathering speed.

Indiana thought for a moment about leaping the gap and taking Ringo on, but this would mean becoming separated from Aisha – never an option. Ringo had won this particular

battle and Indiana knew it. The big, foolish goon waved bye-bye as his part of the train headed on towards Turkey.

Ringo was rather pleased with himself. For once in his life, he'd carried out a plan successfully. Perhaps he would be rewarded with a little slice of delicious treasure. He liked the idea of this, and he smiled to himself.

Indiana Bones felt quite the opposite. He and Aisha were now stuck in the dark countryside with no means of continuing their journey or reaching Dr Ghatak in time. What on earth were they going to do?

11

Old Meg

Indiana rushed back to Aisha, arriving with a skid in front of his friend. 'Major problem,' he whispered in her ear. 'Ringo was on this train and he's uncoupled our carriage. We're stuck in the middle of nowhere.'

Around them, people began to realise the

problem. 'I just looked out of the window,' one passenger shouted. 'The front of the train has gone on without us. I saw it pulling away.'

Other passengers were standing up now, peering into the darkness. One of the train guards arrived from his sleeping quarters at the end of their carriage. He had pulled an emergency cord, which had activated a red flashing light in the carriage, and was talking on a phone. 'Stay in your seats, ladies and gentlemen,' he said. 'There is a problem with the train and we need to get you all back to Budapest, where we will make arrangements for the next part of your journey.'

Aisha looked at Bones and they nodded at each other, knowing exactly what they needed

to do. As soon as the guard moved up to the end of the carriage, Aisha grabbed her bag and they both slipped unnoticed off the train. There was no way they were heading back to Budapest.

Outside, in the darkness, in the middle of nowhere, the enormity of their predicament began to sink in. When they were safely away from the railway track, Aisha turned to her friend. 'How was Ringo even on the train? How did he know? How long was he following us?'

'Since we left Julimus's flat,' said Indiana, sheepishly.

'WHAAAT?' replied Aisha in disbelief. 'And you didn't even think to tell me?'

'I didn't know right away!' Indiana

explained. 'He was disguised as a blonde woman. I was on to *her*, but I had no idea it was *him*. I couldn't risk talking to you – there were so many people in the carriage.'

'Gaaah!' said Aisha, exasperated. 'What are we going to do? How are we going to get to Turkey? We must be a thousand miles away!'

'There's a town down there, said Indiana, looking towards some twinkly lights below them in the dark. 'Maybe we can get a taxi to the next big city.'

It was half a plan. Half a rubbish plan, to be exact, but with no other ideas they began to scramble quickly down the hillside.

When they reached the town, they scurried around searching for something, someone,

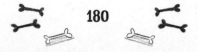

anything that could help them. They quickly found two things:

- The little town was called Novi Žednik.
- Novi Žednik was way too small to have a taxi firm.

The only things of note were a closed post office and an immaculately kept football pitch next to a river. They sat down on a bench on the side of the football pitch. Aisha thought of the pitch on top of Julimus's apartment, where she had argued with her dad, and a tear trickled down her face. She had let him down. He was in grave danger and she had

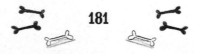

failed to help. It was cold, it was the middle of the night and she was in the middle of rural Serbia.

She slipped a hand in her pocket to search for a hanky. Instead, she felt something unfamiliar, which she pulled out. It was the business card she'd been given the day before.

Bureau of Missing International Artefacts

DIMITAR VAKONDEMBER

Budapest,
Széchenyi István tér 7,
1051 Hungary

T - 0036 771 84395
M - 07861 494 1000

She showed it to Indiana. 'It's the man I played chess with,' she said. 'We could try calling him.'

'The guy who hates children, dogs and archaeologists?' replied Indiana.

'I know,' said Aisha. 'But right now, Mr Vakondember is literally our only hope.'

'What will you say?' Indiana asked.

'I have no idea,' she replied.

'It's the middle of the night,' said Indiana. 'He'll be even grumpier than usual.'

'Thanks for that,' Aisha gulped.

She took out her phone, tapped in the number and waited, with the fingers on her free hand crossed for luck. The phone rang and rang and rang. She had almost given up hope when a sleepy voice answered in Hungarian.

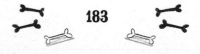

'*Szia.*'

'Er, hello, Mr Vakondember. This is Aisha, the girl you played chess with on the train.'

'Good heavens!' replied Mr Vakondember. 'It's the middle of the night, child. Why are you calling me now?'

'I am so sorry, sir. It's an emergency. We have become separated from the train and are stranded somewhere in Serbia. There is much I did not tell you when we met. My dog and I are travelling to Istanbul to try and rescue my father. He is in great danger.'

'Why don't you contact the local police?' Mr Vakondember asked, perfectly reasonably.

'I can't call the police because ...' She paused to think of a fib, but decided that she

might as well just tell the truth. Time was running out. 'The man I believe to be a threat to my father is called Lord Henry Lupton. He is very rich and well connected. He may even be able to control the police.'

There was a long pause. Then . . .

'Did you say *Lord Henry Lupton*?' Mr Vakondember asked in a voice full of quiet rage.

Aisha was taken aback at his tone. 'Yes,' she replied.

'We know him as the Serpent. The Bureau of Missing International Artefacts has been trying to catch him for longer than I can remember,' exclaimed Mr Vakondember. 'Who is your father?'

'His name is Satnam Ghatak,' Aisha answered.

'This is incredible!' stuttered Mr Vakondember. 'Remember I told you that I hated all archaeologists apart from one? That one is your father! We at the bureau hold Dr Ghatak in the highest regard. I would crawl a mile over broken glass to help him – ten if it also meant catching the Serpent. Tell me, child, where are you?'

Aisha felt a small glimmer of hope in her tummy. 'We're in a place called Novi Žednik, which has a rather fine football pitch. We are there.'

'I'll be with you as soon as I can,' replied Mr Vakondember swiftly, and with that he was gone.

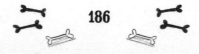

'Wow,' said Aisha. 'That I did not expect.'

'What did he say?' asked Indiana.

Aisha was still trying to understand all that she had heard.

'Well?' Indiana urged.

'Well ... to cut a long story short, Mr Vakondember knows and hates Lupton, and he knows and loves Dad. How unlikely is that? And he said he'll be here as soon as he can.'

Indiana Bones scratched his head. For a magical talking dog from another dimension, the weird and wonderful world of humans was often difficult to understand.

Still not quite believing their change of luck, they sat down to wait. Aisha unzipped her bag. 'I have four aloo parathas, two Babybels

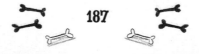

187

and the rest of the fizzy peaches. Would you like something?'

'Confirmative,' said Indiana Bones.

'Let's share,' said Aisha, handing out the last of the food. Eating helped to cheer them up a bit.

'What would you eat if you could have anything you wanted right now?' Indiana asked.

'A huge plate of Edith's buttery crumpets and a pot of hot tea,' Aisha said, without even having to think. 'What about you?'

Indiana paused, giving the matter great consideration. This was pretty much his favourite game and each time his answer was different. 'Fifty-five fish fingers, four Fantas and a bowl of Frosties,' he replied.

'Epic,' said Aisha. 'And you'd also be

welcome to share my crumpets if you were still hungry,' she added. Our scruffy hero smiled, then stood and cocked an ear to the sky, and sniffed at the heavens.

'Here we go,' he said. 'Something's coming.'

Aisha stood and they looked high into the sky. It was still dark, but dawn was approaching and the distant horizon was becoming bronze, orange and yellow in colour. At first, they could only hear a soft rumble, but after a few moments they were rewarded with a light coming towards them. As it got closer, the light became two lights, and they saw it was two huge lamps at the front of an enormous flying machine. What was it? An airship? Some kind of plane?

As it drew nearer, Aisha and Indiana saw that it was not like any plane they had seen before. It glided over the river and trees and touched down on the football pitch, wobbling to a halt right in front of them.

The aircraft was a phenomenal-looking beast. The wooden body seemed to have been constructed out of an old boat, with long panels painted black, and little brass porthole windows, like you would see on a ship. The wings were a skeleton of wooden poles with leather stretched over them, and were shaped like the wings of a pterodactyl, or maybe a fifty-foot bat.

The front was semicircular with many glass windows, lit from within. Inside, the captain

of this incredible craft removed his flying helmet and goggles. He ran his hands through his hair, looked down and nodded an awkward hello at them. Then a rope ladder unfurled silently from a trap door below the cockpit, and Mr Vakondember descended quickly to greet them.

'Zoink-a-doodle-doo,' said Aisha, almost speechless.

'This,' said Mr Vakondember, 'is Old Meg.'

'That's Old Meg!' gasped Aisha. 'You actually invented this?'

Mr Vakondember blushed. 'Invented her and built her. As I said, it's my passion. I am proud to work for the bureau, but my soul craves something – how shall I put it? – a little more

creative. I have been working on Old Meg for twenty years and, as you can see, she is now fully operational.'

'She certainly is,' said Aisha, walking round his amazing creation.

'As I understand it, time is of the essence,' said Mr Vakondember earnestly. 'Climb in and we'll set off. You can tell me everything I need to know on the way.'

They all scrambled up the ladder and into the cockpit of Old Meg, where they strapped themselves into surprisingly comfy seats. After he had done the necessary safety checks, Mr Vakondember taxied to the far end of the football pitch and turned Old Meg around. He pulled out the throttle, the engine let out

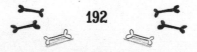

a beefy roar, and the fabulous flying machine bounced along the ground before climbing clumsily back into the sky, setting a course for the magical city of Ephesus.

12

Sirkeci Station

So, my lovely page-sniffing, paragraph-tickling book gobblers, I suspect that you may have been wondering how Dr Ghatak was doing on his two-thousand-mile mega-journey. The answer is that he was doing very well indeed, but I am afraid to say that at Sirkeci station, that was about to change.

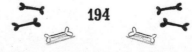

Dawn was breaking in Turkey. The journey so far had been very pleasant for Dr Ghatak. He and Celia had read books, chittered and chatted, and snoozed and snacked, enjoying each other's company. Just as planned, Celia had left the train in Bulgaria to meet her clients, and Dr Ghatak had remained on board until its final stop, Istanbul.

As the train trundled towards the end of its journey, our favourite silver-haired archaeologist was dreaming about treasure. He loved hunting for it, he loved finding it, but most of all he loved sharing it with the world, and these were passions he'd passed on to Aisha. It was his turn to wonder how many schools, libraries and hospitals he

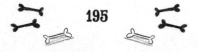

could help to build when they found the Avenger's loot.

Like his daughter, the famous archaeologist travelled light, with just a small backpack for essential items, which meant that his arms were free and he could walk purposefully. At Istanbul he alighted quickly and moved with intent along the crowded platform. The polished marble floor and Dr Ghatak's shoes combined to make a click-clackety sound, as though a clock was measuring out the time it took to make his exit.

Along one wall of the main station building were a dozen arched double doors, each with a large circular stained-glass window above. Dr Ghatak chose the nearest and breezed

through to find that here too it was packed with people.

Architecturally, the space was stunning. The busy bustle of people bounced off the walls and ceiling, making it feel like a cavernous concert hall before a great performance. The walls were cream-coloured, with smoky pink-painted columns and rafters, and the round stained-glass windows above the double doors spilled shards of pretty colours that spliced the space with dazzling daggers of blue, green and red light.

At the station's main door there was a crowd of taxi and bus drivers holding up signs displaying the names of the people they were supposed to collect. Satnam Ghatak was on

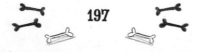

the lookout for Dr Aziz, the elderly driver who had been organised by Charman and Dukes to collect him.

Finally, he spotted his own name, written on a piece of white card:

DR GHATAK

He waved to the driver and walked over. This was definitely not the old Dr Aziz that he had been expecting. He was a man, for starters, and looked about twenty-five years old behind his dark glasses. He had very short black hair and was dressed in a sandy-coloured suit. Dr Ghatak wondered if he was Dr Aziz's son.

'Come, sir,' said the driver. 'My car is very close by.'

As they exited the station, Dr Ghatak's instincts told him that something was not right. 'So, you're not the usual driver ...' he began.

'He is sick today,' said the new guy. 'I'm covering for him.'

Satnam Ghatak knew now that this was a trap. Mr Charman had clearly told him that Dr Aziz was a retired woman.

'Oh dear,' he said casually. 'We'd already agreed on a price. Are you one of his colleagues?'

'Yes,' said the driver. 'Don't worry, the price will be the same.'

'Well, you must pass young Mr Aziz my best wishes when you see him,' said Dr Ghatak, not letting on that the man had been rumbled while he thought about what to do. 'I hope *he* gets better soon.'

'Of course,' replied the new driver.

It was time for what Dr Ghatak called evasive action. He noticed they'd just walked past an alley, which had steep steps leading down to the left. Up ahead was another similar-looking alley. As they drew level with it, Dr Ghatak gave the driver a hefty shove, which sent him flying down an identical staircase.

Dr Ghatak took flight. He dashed across the road, weaving in and out of traffic. A car

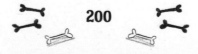

screeched to a halt just in front of him and he rolled over its bonnet. Horns honked hard as the impatient Istanbul traffic ground to a halt. The archaeologist leaped up and sprinted towards a busy marketplace, where he hoped that he could disappear into the crowds before the young driver could recover himself.

Dr Ghatak ran at full tilt. He knew the decoy driver was fitter and faster, but Satnam hoped that he was cleverer. Turning into a small park, he slowed to a brisk walk, passing picnickers and a juggler dressed as a pirate.

In the corner of the park was another flight of stairs leading up the side of a building. As Dr Ghatak disappeared up them, two at a time, his pursuer appeared at the gates. Like an efficient

search droid, he made an examination of the park. No Ghatak. He spotted the stairs and walked swiftly towards them.

By now, Dr Ghatak had reached the top and was up on the city walls, with row after row of red-tiled rooftops stretching out beyond him. He looked across Istanbul and saw the majestic Hagia Sophia mosque, which dominated the skyline with its enormous dome and minarets. He saw boats on the Bosphorus and thought briefly about heading for Ephesus the old-fashioned way, by water.

Walking swiftly along walls and along the ridges of rooftops, dodging around TV aerials and solar panels, he hopped from one building to another, heading towards what

he hoped was the city's centre. Dr Ghatak felt vulnerable up here and wished he was back on the ground, where he could blend in with the heaving crowds.

Looking over his shoulder, he saw the young driver still in hot pursuit. He was talking into a mobile phone. No doubt calling for backup.

This was not good. Dr Ghatak began to jog gently, while keeping a close eye on the sandy-suited fellow. The man following him was so confident that he would catch up he did not feel the need to run. His professional training had told him rooftops offer very few places to hide.

Dr Ghatak knew this too, but kept up a steady jog. Then he spotted something

interesting ahead. It was a vast rectangle of a building, as big as fifteen football pitches. Its roof was covered in fifteen enormous domes. Satnam had never seen it from above, but he suspected that this was the roof of Istanbul's Grand Bazaar, a huge indoor market with over four thousand shops spread over sixty-one covered streets. If he could somehow get inside, looking for him would be like trying to find a noodle in a haystack.

As this thought dawned on Dr Ghatak, it did too on sandy-suit, who now began to sprint. Satnam took a huge leap across a gap and landed, only just on the roof of the bazaar. Running in and out of the domes, he spotted an open window vent and crawled inside. Like

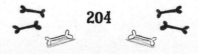

a gymnast, he swung from rung to rung on the old metal ladder he found there. He traversed the inside of the dome, with hundreds of unaware shoppers below him, before dropping silently down onto a pile of carpets at a rug stall.

At ground level, Dr Ghatak felt much safer, even though on looking up, he saw that his follower was taking the exact same route. Our favourite Oxford-based archaeologist smiled as he slipped into the surrounding throng.

Blending in with all the shoppers, Dr Ghatak pulled a roll of Turkish banknotes from his inside jacket pocket. At the next stall he hastily purchased a black-and-white baseball cap bearing the crest of Beşiktaş, one of Istanbul's big three football teams. He removed his

jacket and made his way into the depths of the market. He was now a white-shirted man with a cap, rather than a sharp-suited gentleman with shoulder-length silver hair. He found a small cafe and slipped inside, taking a table at the back.

Coffee ordered, he breathed a sigh of relief. *Still got it, Satnam,* he smiled to himself. Just between you and me, Dr Ghatak was feeling rather smug at having escaped from what he assumed was a professionally trained bounty hunter half his age.

His happiness was short-lived, however, as the proprietor of the cafe approached his table, carrying a large black telephone. 'For you,' he said.

Dr Ghatak was confuzzled, thinking the man had made a mistake, but he took the receiver anyway. 'Hello?'

'Ah, Dr Ghatak,' a voice slithered. 'Excellent work in evading my associate, who is most annoyed. One hundred points to you. However, ten thousand points to me for finding you again so easily.'

Satnam was startled, but immediately guessed who it was. 'Lupton? How did you know I was here?'

'As soon as I heard you'd crashed into the bazaar, I contacted the head of security there. He is an old friend. He checked his security cameras, and that brings us all nicely up to date with how excellent I am,' wheezed the oily villain.

'So what do you want?'

'I have someone here who would very much like to say a quick hi,' whispered the venomous voice.

To Dr Ghatak's horror, Celia's voice came on the line. 'I'm so sorry, Satnam,' she stuttered. 'They kidnapped me at the station in Bulgaria. They say they are going to lock me up unless you give them what they want.'

'Don't worry, Celia, I'll get you out of this,' Dr Ghatak said, but he had no idea if she heard as next moment her vile captor was back on the line.

'There is only one way that you can help, Dr Ghatak. If you wish to see Celia again, get yourself to Atatürk airport. We will be waiting

for you at the private jet terminal. A plane will take us to Ephesus, where you will take us to the lost treasure of the Lonely Avenger. Then, and only then, will you both be released.'

Dr Ghatak had no choice. He loved treasure. He loved hunting for it and he loved finding it, but he loved people a million times more. So Satnam Ghatak paid for his coffee and went outside to look for a taxi.

13

The Temple of Diana

So, dearly beloved readers, at this point in our story we had two quite different aircraft up in the air at the same time, both headed for the same destination. One was a sleek supersonic

jet belonging to the sssslithery sssSerpent, transporting Celia and Dr Ghatak, both securely handcuffed, and Lupton, Philip Castle and Ringo, fresh from his heroics aboard Aisha's train. The other aircraft was Old Meg, which was slower and less sleek than the jet, but a hundred times cooler, looking as it did like a cross between a bird, a boat and a bat.

'So,' began the Serpent to Dr Ghatak, 'where exactly are we going when we reach Ephesus?'

'The Temple of Diana,' said Dr Ghatak stonily.

'You heard the man,' the Serpent hissed to the pilot, who set his coordinates accordingly for a small private airstrip near to the ancient ruins.

The Serpent licked his thin dry lips in anticipation of what might lie ahead. On a tablet he called up an image of the temple, tilting it proudly for people to see, as if somehow he was the owner of the colossal, gleaming white marble temple that dwarfed everything around it.

'Incredible,' said the stubbly-chinned Castle.

'You could buy it when you get your hands on the treasure!' said Ringo.

'*Estúpido idiota!*' snapped Castle. 'That was what it looked like a thousand years ago! It's a heap of rubble now.'

Ringo slumped back in his seat, embarrassed, wondering why anyone would want to buy a heap of rubble.

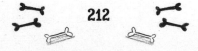

Luckily the flight wasn't long and soon the pilot began preparations for their descent. Once on the ground, the passengers disembarked quickly into a waiting jeep that would take them to the site of the once beautiful temple.

During the drive, Lupton forced Dr Ghatak to explain how the temple featured in the search for the Avenger's treasure, greedy for this man's knowledge as well as the loot. He was very pleased with what he heard.

'Very good,' the Serpent grinned, licking his spindly lips. 'The treasure shall be found and shall be mine.'

Castle was not as pleased to hear this. *Ours*, he protested in his head, but didn't say it out loud. He was beginning to wonder if Lupton

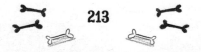

would make good his promise to share the bounty with him.

Satnam did not like Lupton one bit, and even though he was helpless to do anything, he felt his anger building. 'Greedy men who spend their lives stealing, chasing children and making them fear for their lives will eventually be caught,' he said.

'Oh boo-hoo,' teased Lupton. 'You have no idea who you are dealing with.'

'I do though,' chipped in Celia. 'I know who you are and I know exactly how you have amassed your wealth – by taking it from other people. But now you've crawled out from under your rock, the net around you is beginning to close.'

Lupton ignored her, addressing only Dr

214

Ghatak. 'You will regret crossing me,' he said. 'Once you have given me what I need, I will crush you, and your stupid daughter will be placed in an orphanage.'

'And you'll never see your dim dog again,' added Ringo, his confidence buoyed by the excellent diversion job he had done on Aisha and Indiana Bones.

Dr Ghatak leaned back in his seat, squeezing Celia's hand, wishing desperately that they were both safe at home in Oxford.

At last, the jeep pulled up next to a field with a solitary column in the middle, all that remained of the once majestic Temple of Diana.

'What now?' said Philip Castle as they got out of the jeep.

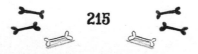

'If you uncuff me, I can begin,' Dr Ghatak answered.

Lupton, Castle and Ringo stared round at the scruffy field. 'But there's nothing here,' said Castle.

'Patience,' slithered Lupton. 'Uncuff him and let him do his job.'

Ringo pulled a key out and released Dr Ghatak, who began to walk the site, rubbing at his wrists. He climbed a little slope to survey the area, then, bending down, he opened his backpack and pulled out a black bag which looked a bit like a folding camping chair.

'What's that?' asked Lupton.

'This is a GPR machine,' Dr Ghatak answered, beginning to assemble the device.

'It stands for **G**round **P**enetrating **R**adar. It will tell us exactly what is below us to a depth of forty metres and send an image back to the screen. If there is anything interesting beneath this field, we'll find out.'

'How long will it take?' asked Castle urgently.

'Maybe an hour,' Dr Ghatak answered.

The Serpent's eyes lit up. 'Well then,' he said. 'You'd better get started.'

High in the sky, and not a million miles away, Old Meg was wobbling towards Ephesus like a paper plane sellotaped to a bumblebee.

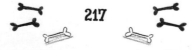

217

On board, Aisha and Indiana Bones sat in the semicircular glass cockpit with Dimitar Vakondember. Just as her father had explained to Lupton, Aisha too was explaining why they thought that the treasure of the Lonely Avenger was hidden somewhere near the Temple of Diana.

'How exciting!' said Dimitar from behind the controls of the wondrous flying machine. 'If I am a part of the discovery of this treasure, I shall be able to retire from the Bureau of Missing International Artefacts a hero and spend all of my time inventing. I can continue my work on Underwater Meg – a submarine. What do you think of that?'

'Sounds wonderful. We can look for treasure

under the sea,' Aisha beamed.

Their chitter-chatter was interrupted by a ping from her phone. 'Cool! It's an email from Julimus,' she announced and began to read it aloud.

Indiana, still pretending that he was not a magical talking dog from Skara Brae, listened keenly.

Dear Ms Aisha Ghatak and Mr Indiana Bones,

I hope this email finds you both well and that you are close to being reunited with your father. I fear that I must tell you immediately that I am writing to you with a very heavy heart.

It is bad news about our dear departed friend, the Lonely Avenger. If you remember, I told you that the knight had landed in Alexandria and had fallen in love again – with books. He tried to rebuild his life in the library, where he immersed himself in stories from the four corners of the world, and studied philosophy, art, religion and science.

It seems he was very happy, but then tragedy struck our friend once more. Just as the Avenger had found some peace and happiness, the library at Alexandria was destroyed by fire. For the third time in his life, the thing that he loved the most was taken from him.

'Oh no, the poor knight!' said Aisha. 'I just want to give him a big hug.' She continued to read.

It seems all I am able to give you is a sad story of love and loss. I know from the last page I scanned that the Avenger, devastated once more, racked with grief, got back aboard the *Black Tiger* and left. I am sorry that I have nothing of use to say about the treasure.

Please contact me when you are safely reunited with your father. Good luck.

Your friend,

Julimus

Indiana curled up and put his chin on his paws. He felt so sad for the Avenger, who'd now lost Diane, Amie his dog, and his library. He tried to put himself in the shoes of the tragic knight. What would he have done after his library had burned down? Where would he have gone next? The dog closed his eyes and, as he did so, the sapphire in his collar began to glow, meaning strange forces were at work. With Indiana in a trance-like state, images and pictures from centuries ago began to float through his mind. He dreamed a dream of the old knight, and his visions swam with words and pages from the journal, and fire and tears and sunrise.

*

Back on the ground at the temple, Dr Ghatak had completed a full sweep of the site and returned to the Serpent and Castle disappointed. 'There's nothing here,' he said. 'Below us is only very dense stone. There are no chambers or buried artefacts. Nothing at all.'

'NO!' spat Lupton, instantly furious.

'I'm sorry,' said Satnam, packing away his GPR machine. 'I cannot find what is not there. Our theory was incorrect. It was always a possibility.'

'Then I shall have you both thrown into a dungeon for the rest of your days!' raged the Serpent, kicking Dr Ghatak's backpack and making it fizz along the ground.

'There are people who know what you are up to, Mr Lupton,' warned Celia. 'I have associates who know what sort of games you play. If we go missing, the authorities will swarm all over you.'

'I own the authorities, you foolish woman,' said Lupton without a care, almost as if Celia were a crumb he was flicking off a table.

'It could take months to discover a new lead in the search for the treasure,' Dr Ghatak told the Serpent, but Lord Henry Lupton was fresh out of patience.

'Well, you'll have plenty of time to work on that when you are locked up somewhere nasty with nothing else to distract you,' he seethed.

Lupton's furious threat was interrupted

by a deep chugging noise from above. High in the sky, Old Meg was approaching. Mr Vakondember brought her in to circle the area. Looking out of the brightly lit cockpit was Aisha, who waved delightedly at her father.

Satnam waved too – but frantically, desperate that she should not land and get herself captured by these terrible people.

'How on earth did that brat get here?' fumed the Serpent. 'Whenever treasure is afoot, she turns up like a bad penny.' Lupton rounded on Ringo. 'I thought you'd taken care of her, you pungent, pitiful pillock?'

'I did ... I had ... she was ...' Ringo stammered in disbelief, looking up at Mr Vakondember's incredible aeroplane.

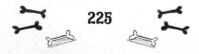

Dimitar Vakondember heeded Satnam's warning and steered Old Meg away from the site of the ruined temple. Looking out of the window to the west, he spotted the main ruins of the ancient city of Ephesus and pointed them out to Aisha. As he did so, Indiana Bones sat bolt upright, wide awake once more.

He extended his paw, rolled out a solitary claw and used it to beckon Aisha over. She could see that the jewel in Indiana's collar was blinking like a beacon, so she went over and knelt next to her friend.

'The knight did not hide his treasure where your father is looking,' he whispered. The sapphire buzzed as the magical dog closed his eyes again and pictured the Avenger. He could

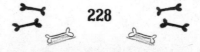

see clearly where the knight was and, more importantly, what he was surrounded by. 'You need to ask Mr Vakondember to land the plane right in the middle of Ephesus. I know *exactly* where we should look for the Avenger and his treasure.'

Were they on the cusp of something delicious and funbelievable? The answer, my friends, is yes, they were. What they were about to discover in Ephesus would blow this adventure sky high.

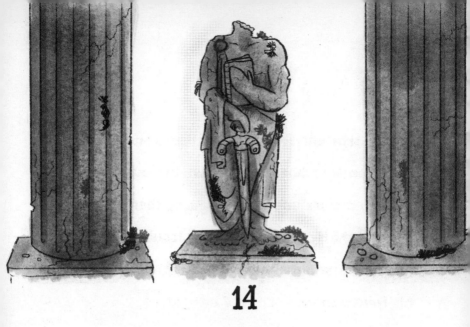

14

Hairy Hero on a Mega Mission

The Serpent's small dark eyes glared after Old

Meg. Our villainous villain licked his thin snaky

lips as Dimitar Vakondember's homemade

flying machine trundled away. Lupton had a

feeling that the little girl on board, who had been one step ahead of him at the pyramids, was more than one step ahead of them again right now. He would not and could not be beaten to the treasure by a child.

'Follow that ... THING!' he spat.

At the Serpent's word, his team bundled Dr Ghatak and Celia into the jeep. With a screech of tyres and a cloud of dust, they sped off in pursuit of our formidable heroes.

Circling above the ancient ruins, Dimitar Vakondember was looking for a safe place to land. A row of marble columns in various stages of collapse caught his eye, lining what would have been a long street above the ruined city's centre. Skilfully, he brought the plane

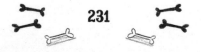

down. Old Meg's batlike wings were just short enough for him to land safely without clipping any of the ancient columns.

Climbing down from the aircraft, Aisha looked around in awe at her new surroundings. It was now very late afternoon and the last visitor had left Ephesus for the day. There is something quite wonderful about being somewhere beautiful when all the crowds have gone home. Within moments she had fallen in love with the unbelievably well preserved Roman city. Bathed in soft light, Ephesus looked calm and magical, and Aisha felt very lucky to be there. But she couldn't relax just yet.

'Mr Vakondember, I am worried that the men holding my father could soon be here.

Would you keep a safe distance from us?'
Aisha asked. 'We may need your help if we
are captured.'

'Of course,' he replied.

Reassured, Aisha and Bones began to make
their way along the street. Around them, small
clumps of brilliant red poppies grew out of the
dry earth, adding wonderful dashes of deep
colour in stunning contrast to the white marble
stone, the predominant building material of the
ancient city.

Further along, Aisha could see a huge
Roman outdoor theatre, which also was dotted
with thousands of red poppies. She longed to
explore every single corner of this special place,
but Indiana's thoughts were consumed with the

vision of the knight he'd had. He was sniffing away at the ground, heading down the gentle slope that seemed to lead towards the centre of Ephesus.

Our hairy hero was on a mega mission and next moment he was off, like a mighty cannon ball. Aisha barely noticed him go, still hypnotised by the surroundings. As she looked around, she saw to her delight that the only other visitors to the ancient city were tortoises. For Aisha, the presence of these creatures added extra magic. She loved the idea that generation after generation of tortoises must have lived in Ephesus.

She came to her senses hearing Indiana's claws skittering on the ancient stones as he

tried to maintain his grip. Aisha began to jog to catch up with her pal, passing the ruins of a building which had clearly once been a Roman bath house. She jogged on downhill, past fallen temples and mighty fountains, their white marble standing out against the deep blue of the Turkish sky.

Aisha was now making her way along what had once been the city's largest street. There were the ruins of rows of shops, maybe once tailors, fishmongers, bakers, butchers and greengrocers. Behind were tumbledown terraced houses, some still showing the remains of colourfully tiled interiors, where the wealthier citizens of the city would have lived and laughed and loved.

Aisha stared out towards the horizon and remembered her father telling her that in the knight's day, the sea would have come right up into the city. She tried to conjure up a vision of the busy port and picture the *Black Tiger* moored there.

Indiana was already at the bottom of the hill. 'Wait for me!' Aisha shouted, skipping along the same paving stones that the Ephesians had trodden on thousands of years ago.

Bones was standing with his tail and ears pointing up, super alert. He had found what he was looking for and was waiting in front of the city's grandest building. The jewel in Ephesus's crown was an architectural marvel. The front

of the building was extremely well preserved. There were two storeys of intricately carved marble with sixteen enormous columns, eight on the ground floor and another eight on what would have been the second floor. Indiana stood, silent as a statue, staring up at the building's incredible facade as Aisha arrived beside him.

'Wow!' she said. 'What is it?'

'It's the library,' Indiana answered, cool as a snowman's choc ice. 'I saw a picture of it in a book at Julimus's. I don't think the Avenger wasn't interested in the Temple of Diana. He loved books. If he was ever in Ephesus, this is where he would have come.'

'Gosh! Clever Indiana Bones,' Aisha nodded. 'Of course, he came here!'

'Confirmative,' said Indiana. 'He lost one library and found another.'

'Who's my pal!' said Aisha, bending down to cuddle her number one friend.

'Let's look for clues,' he whispered back, which made Aisha's eyes dance with excitement.

Indiana and Aisha made a careful circuit of the library, studying the hieroglyphics and the ancient texts on the outside. It wasn't long before Aisha spotted the mark of the Avenger above a block of ancient text. 'Indiana! Look, here!'

Indiana looked at the strange text, and Aisha began to read and translate. It was written in Ottoman Turkish, which Aisha

238

was very familiar with, thanks to her archaeological training.

> *A true friend in times of sorrow*
> *Thought and wisdom here to borrow*
> *All of knowledge found inside*
> *In which book will the next clue hide?*
> *Be brave of thought, rested, agree*
> *You are never alone when you're*
> > *with me.*

A true friend in times of sorrow – those words had been in one of Julimus's emails!

Indiana danced. 'It's a message from the Avenger. He is talking about books!'

In which book will the next clue hide? Aisha

read again. 'We need to find a picture of a book!'

The pair of them began to race around the ancient library looking for pictures of books carved into the stone. Gaaaaaah – there were hundreds! This would take until five past forever.

Aisha checked out as many of them as she could, running her fingers over the stonework, looking for anything that might give them a further clue. Indiana did the same with his paws and his hairy hooter.

'Aisha!' he called after a few minutes. 'Come, quick.'

At the front of the building were four pairs of columns, and in an alcove between each pair

was a statue. They'd not paid much attention to the statues when they had first arrived, but now they examined them and saw that they represented different virtues: Thought, Knowledge, Bravery and Wisdom.

Indiana pointed to one of the ancient marble figures. It had no head, but ... 'Look at its sword, Aisha!'

Aisha looked. The sword looked exactly like the one they had found inside the Great Pyramid of Khufu.

'It's the Avenger's sword!' gasped Aisha.

In the statue's other hand was a small book. Aisha began to run her fingers around the book, looking for something, anything. Her heart stopped when she found a tiny hole. The

only finger she could fit inside the hole was her little finger, so she jiggled it inside and wiggled it around. Suddenly, this little piggy went to market and struck gold, literally! Inside the hole was a small golden lever.

With her little finger, she pulled the lever as hard as she could and from behind the library facade came a slow grinding sound. Aisha and Indiana rushed to investigate and found that a small opening had appeared. It was just big enough for a child and a magical dog to squish through.

Indiana Bones and Aisha Ghatak squeezed themselves through. What happened when they got inside was more incredible than either of them could have dreamed. I am the

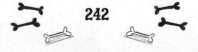

captain of this book and even I am struggling to know how to begin to talk about it. I need to take a break before I begin, and maybe you should too.

15

The Greatest Gift

As soon as Indiana and Aisha had squeezed themselves through the gap, they found themselves in near total darkness. Aisha's heart pounded, and our heroes' sapphires blinked and blazed and beamed like the bright lights on top of an emergency vehicle.

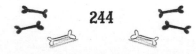

244

Were they really about to find the lost treasure of the Lonely Avenger that had remained hidden for centuries?

Aisha pulled a torch from her backpack and shone it around. They walked gingerly along the passageway and found themselves at the top of a steep staircase. It was much lighter here, so Aisha switched off the torch. Looking down the stairs, she could see the walls were lined with candle lanterns. 'Look, Indiana,' she said. 'These candles look as though they have just been lit a minute ago. They're brand new. Doesn't that seem impossible to you?'

Indiana was a dog from a different dimension and he knew that many things were possible. He'd started his life in a strange

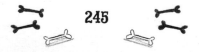

underground chamber frozen in time, and this place he'd never been to before felt so familiar. In fact, Indiana Bones suddenly had the weirdest feeling that he was somehow coming home.

Indiana and Aisha's sapphires buzzed, sparkled and crackled electric blue.

'Tread carefully, Aisha. Ancient and deep magic is at work here,' said Bones, sniffing the cold air and edging closer to his friend.

They followed the everlasting candles down the staircase and through a maze of tunnels until they came to a passageway which had a door at the end. On the door was painted a phrase in ancient symbols, which Aisha read:

A true friend in times of sorrow

Aisha's heart boomed.

'Well?' Indiana asked.

'Well, what?' Aisha said.

'Shall we go in?'

'I don't know,' she whispered. 'It feels as though we should be super quiet. Just in case.'

'Well, we are in a library,' Indiana chuckled.

Aisha knocked gently, then pushed the door open. 'Hello – is anyone here?'

They were both startled when Aisha's question was answered by a thin and reedy voice. 'Don't just stand there,' it said. 'Come in.'

Indiana and Aisha looked at one another, then stepped through the doorway. They found themselves in a small, simple study with red walls, lit by more everlasting candle lamps. They both gasped, recognising the room from the dream they'd shared in Julimus's apartment. At one end was a large wooden reading table, strewn with books and scrolls and paper and quills, and a vase full of freshly picked, blood-red poppies.

A little old man was sitting at the table. Aisha thought that he looked like a monk, dressed as he was in simple brown robes and leather slippers embroidered with golden stars.

'Sorry to disturb you, sir,' said Aisha. 'I think we may have taken a wrong turn or something . . .' She tailed off.

The monk looked up from his book. 'No,

Aisha, you are in the right place. I have been expecting you. It's good that you are finally here.'

'What? How do you know my name?' Aisha asked. 'Who are you?'

Even as she said this, she started to understand. Being a magical dog, Indiana was ahead of her and he stepped forward.

'This is the Lonely Avenger, Aisha. It's good to meet you at last, sir,' he said, bowing his head. 'We've seen you in our dreams, but it's so much better to meet you in person.'

'It is indeed,' smiled the old man. 'And my dreams told me of you, the dog who is able to talk. I too have one of those.'

From under the table, a dog's head popped

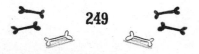

up. She skittered into view, wagging her tail. 'Hello, everybody.'

'Amie! You found her!' said Aisha.

Indiana Bones froze. The sapphire in his collar was shining so brightly, he could feel it almost burning the skin around his neck. He crouched down and the two dogs gently, carefully sniffed each other. Indiana sat up suddenly. It couldn't be? Could it?

'Mum?' Indiana asked nervously.

'It IS you!' said Amie. 'It's REALLY you!'

If the knight was surprised, he hid it well, but his enormous smile gave away how he felt. As he twinkled, he looked twenty years younger, and he began to laugh. 'This is wonderful, Amie. It's your long-lost boy, your son!'

Aisha was so happy to see this reunion that tears began to roll down her cheeks. 'But how can this be?' she asked.

The knight beamed at Aisha. 'When you and your talking dog came to me in my dreams, I wondered then if our dogs were somehow connected. And now we know — they are mother and son! When I lost my Amie, many years ago, it was because she mistakenly boarded a merchant's ship in Alexandria. She was taken to northern Europe, to a place called Skara Brae, on the Orkney islands in the far north of Scotland. Her magic powers drew her to the attention of the tribal kings, who gave her a home, and she had a large family.

'When Indiana was taken from that magical chamber by your father thousands of years later, my Amie found her way out and travelled the world looking for her son. Ancient magic led her back to me, and now her son has also been drawn here.'

Indiana and his mum gazed lovingly into each other's eyes and nuzzled each other, which felt warm and wonderful.

Aisha and the knight looked at the dogs and grinned at each other. Aisha was weak at the knees with the happiness she felt for Indiana, but then remembered where she was. She bowed her head to the ancient man, though she wasn't sure if this was the right thing to do. It's not every day that you meet

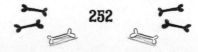

a two-thousand-year-old knight in the magical underground room of an ancient library.

'Your English is good for a French knight,' she said, suddenly feeling self-conscious and tongue-tied.

The Avenger's eyes twinkled. 'I have been studying for many hundreds of years. As you both know, I love to read and have had time to teach myself many languages.'

The calm atmosphere was suddenly interrupted by a rumbling noise deep below them.

'Ah,' said the knight, turning over a large egg timer on his desk. 'How annoying. It has started already. We don't have much time.'

'What do you mean?' Aisha asked.

'When you arrived, the enchantment protecting my reading room was broken – see?' The knight pointed at the poppies on his desk. A moment ago, they had been red and full of life, but they were now turning brown, the petals falling slowly onto the desk. 'What is happening to my poppies will soon be happening to me,' the knight smiled. 'And to my Amie.'

Aisha stared at him in horror. 'No! That's not what we meant to do!'

'We don't want that!' said Indiana, whimpering a little. 'If we'd known, we never would have come. We don't care about the treasure.'

'Ah, my treasure. Excellent!' said the knight. 'Now we can finally get to business.'

'Tell us later – we'd rather get you out safely,' insisted Aisha.

'Dearest girl, we have been hoping for someone like you for an eternity,' smiled the knight. 'It means that we can finally rest, knowing that you two will be able to continue the work that we started.'

'What do you mean?' Aisha said, confused.

But the knight held up his hand. 'My turn for a question. What would you do with the riches that my treasure would bring?'

Aisha answered honestly and without having to think twice. It was the kind of thing she had discussed many times with her father. 'We would build libraries and schools and hospitals.'

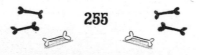

255

'THAT is what I mean!' cried the old knight, clapping his hands. He rose from his chair and crossed the room to a set of shelves. He picked up something small and brought it back to them. Extending his hand, the old man uncurled his closed fist and held out the smallest, most beautiful key that Aisha had ever seen. It was golden, encrusted with diamonds, and sparkled in the candlelight.

'This is for you, my dear,' the knight said. 'It's impossible for anyone to find my treasure without it. I hope it will unlock my fortune for you. I want you to be the ones to find it because I want you to spend it in just the way that you described. I would choose libraries, but schools and hospitals are also most excellent.'

Aisha took the key.

'Now for some more gifts to help you both on your quest. Two things each.'

The knight held something else out to Aisha, but she couldn't see what it was. Reaching out, she felt something hard, metallic and cold – and *completely invisible*.

'This is my shield,' said the knight. 'It will protect you and your friends. Here – let me help you strap it to your back.'

When the invisible shield was safely in place, the knight handed Aisha a small wooden chest. Engraved on a brass plaque were the words: *Arching Bane Compendium de Divino Alchemia.*

'Open it,' said the knight.

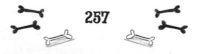

Aisha flicked the catch and carefully lifted the lid. Inside were several rows of tiny jars and crystals, each labelled in some ancient language, with words like:

Viribus   Fortuna   Salutem

'What are these?' Aisha asked, as another deep rumble shook the room.

'No time,' said the knight. 'You will work it out. Indiana will help. Speaking of Indiana, it is your turn for a present,' he said, turning towards our hairy hero.

The Avenger reached to take a leather-bound book from the shelves and handed it to Indiana Bones.

Oh great, Indiana couldn't help thinking. *She gets a super-cool invisi-shield and a chest of magic potions, and I get a book I can't read.*

The knight crouched down to stroke and pet Indiana. 'For you, my friend, my second present is the greatest gift. This should help with the reading.' He stretched his arms over Indiana and waves of colour began to spill from his fingers. Deep crimson, gold and emerald-green light

flooded from the knight and into Indiana Bones.

The scruffy pooch from Skara Brae did not know what was happening to him but he felt amazing. 'What was that?' he asked when the flow eventually stopped.

'That, I hope, was a dream come true,' smiled the knight. 'I have spent thousands of years reading. I can read almost every language, past and present. And I have just transferred all of that ability to you.'

'What?' Indiana asked, a bit shaken. 'I can read properly now?'

'Better than anyone else on the planet,' the knight smiled.

Indiana looked at the cover of the book he had just been given, and he was able not only

to read it, but to translate it also.

'*Arching Bane's Collection of Godlike Knowledge*,' he squealed. Then he tilted his head and frowned a little. 'I can read it, but I still don't know what it means . . .'

He noticed the words on his book were the same as the words on Aisha's potion chest, and the penny finally dropped. 'Hey, Aisha! My book will explain your potions!'

'Very good,' nodded the knight. 'Together with your gifts and the key, you have everything you need to keep yourselves safe, and find what you have been looking for. Now you must go! There is very little time.'

'But we don't know where to look,' said Aisha.

'You have found me twice already. You can find me a third time,' smiled the knight. 'Before I retired to my reading room, I left Ephesus one last time and hid all of my treasure somewhere quite safe. I have lived a rich life. I have loved and lost. I have travelled and been happy. As for the treasure, my dears, here is my clue.

'I did what you would have expected
me to do,
I hid the treasure in the best place in
the world.'

At that moment, the deep rumbling suddenly became much louder.

Aisha glanced at the knight's flowers and

saw that now there was no sign of life left in them at all. The Avenger returned to his chair, and Amie leapt up onto his lap.

'Magic is at work, my love, and we will meet again,' she told her son. 'Now, you must take your Aisha to safety.'

The walls of the red reading room were, like the poppies, losing their colour and beginning to melt into the past, like tears in a sandstorm.

Aisha looked at the knight. He too was beginning to turn slowly to sand, from his embroidered slippers up. The Avenger held out a hand and Aisha grabbed it tightly with both of hers – just for a moment.

'Go, my dears,' said the old man. 'And remember,

'I did what you would have expected

me to do.

I hid the treasure in the best place in

the world.'

As Aisha and Indiana watched, the figures turned to sand right in front of their eyes.

'Go now!' came a final plea. 'And thank you. I am so glad it was you!'

Aisha picked up a handful of the sand and stuffed it into her back pocket. Even in the jaws of danger, she wanted something she could place in a proper grave for this kind old man and his best friend, Amie.

'Now!' said Indiana. Together they flew from the room and fled into the labyrinth of

tunnels and passageways.

As they ran, the world began to disintegrate around them. Aisha held her new shield above them and they ran like the wind, ducking falling timbers and debris, and swerving sections of the tunnel floor which opened up beneath their feet. As they ran past the candles that had led them to the Avenger, one by one the flames went out.

Finally, they saw the stone steps leading up to a sliver of daylight. It wasn't a moment too soon. As the floor fell away behind them, our heroes leaped to the safety of the stairs, taking them two at a time to the top. They shot through the small opening and heard an almighty crack underneath as the magical

cavern disintegrated. Diving for cover behind a large marble statue, they rolled into a ball under the protection of the shield as rocks and stones rained down upon them.

When at last all was quiet, they gingerly emerged from under the shield, hugging each other and feeling a little stunned. Aisha made a futile attempt at dusting herself down, while Indiana shook himself like a wet dog, from the end of his tail to the tip of his nose. Then the pair walked in silence down the steps of the library.

They might have survived the magical underground implosion, but our heroes realised that the danger was far from over. Waiting to greet them at the bottom of the staircase was the

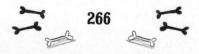

beastly Serpent Lupton, with Castle and stinky Ringo. The only good thing Aisha could see was that her father was also there, alive and well. She was happy, too, to see Celia next to him.

'Well done!' Lupton hissed sarcastically, slow-clapping them mockingly as they approached. 'I am delighted to see that you are both unscathed. Now. Where is the treasure?'

Aisha placed her potions chest and Indiana's book under the invisible shield and rested it all on the floor. Indiana switched into protective mode at Aisha's side, ready to take them all on, but Aisha had had enough of being frightened.

'The treasure is not here, and I don't know where it is,' she told him. 'Just the same as last time, Mr Lupton.'

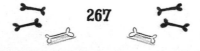

'You can call me MY LORD,' seethed the Serpent, barely able to conceal his anger.

'Either way, Mr Lupton, it's not down there,' said Aisha. 'Do you ever think you could try looking for it yourself? Instead of leaving us to do all the dirty work?'

'Try looking for it? TRY LOOKING FOR IT?' the angry Serpent spewed. His whole body shook with spasms of wrath. His eyes bulged and he turned ruby red with rage. 'I have been looking for FIFTY YEARS! That treasure has been my life and I will not share it with another living soul!'

Castle looked at Lord Henry Lupton and his eyes narrowed as he contemplated something. After a moment, he turned his attention to

Aisha. 'What's in your hand?' he asked, noticing Aisha's tightly closed fist.

'Nothing,' Aisha replied defiantly, annoyed with herself for not concealing the key too.

'Something important then?' slithered the Serpent. 'Give it to me or I can promise you this is the last time you'll see your father and his friend.'

He nodded to Ringo, who stepped menacingly towards the handcuffed Dr Ghatak.

As Aisha and Bones wondered what to do, they heard a voice speak to them out of nowhere.

'Aisha, give them the key. It is just a key. You can get it back when you finally need it. The real key to finding my treasure is the knowledge,

wisdom and understanding that you and Indiana now have.'

The voice of the knight faded away, though only Aisha and Indiana had heard it.

Aisha reluctantly held up the key. 'I found this under the library, with a message that this key will unlock the final resting place of the Avenger's treasure,' she said. 'Release my father and Celia and it's yours. Trick me, and my dog will disappear with the key. Without it, you WILL NEVER get the treasure.'

From above them, a new voice joined the conversation. It was Dimitar Vakondember, and he had filmed everything on his phone. He waved it at the Serpent. 'Do as she asks, Lupton. If you double-cross her, I will have

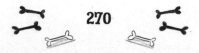

evidence of kidnap.'

The Serpent was now purple with fury. He had no choice but to comply. He ordered Ringo to free Dr Ghatak and Celia and they joyfully rushed over to Aisha and Indiana. Castle took the precious key from Aisha and within a moment the baddies were back in the jeep, speeding away from Ephesus.

Aisha hugged her dad. She was so happy to have him back. Losing the key to the Serpent hurt, but the wellbeing of her father meant more to her than everything.

'Boy, do I have a lot to tell you,' she said. And the proud archaeologist beamed at his incredible daughter.

'I was so frightened,' Celia said. 'You are

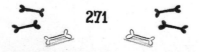

a brave and clever girl.' She opened her arms to Aisha, who without thinking stepped into a cuddle with her too.

'I am so glad you are all safe,' Aisha smiled.

'Now, how the devil are we going to get out of here?' said Dr Ghatak.

'Don't worry,' said Aisha, nodding towards Dimitar Vakondember. 'I think we've got that one covered too. Come on – there's someone who'd very much like to meet you.'

Nearly
The End

Epilogue

So, my most excellent readers, this part of the story is almost done. Dimitar Vakondember took them all back to Budapest, where they were able to catch a train that would take them to Paris and then on to London, and finally home to Oxford.

Aisha and Celia had a good opportunity to talk and to get to know each other a little

more. Dr Ghatak had told Aisha that Celia could be trusted with their family's biggest secret – *Indiana Bones*. 'Would you like to tell her?' he asked with a twinkle.

When the moment was right, and no other people were around, Aisha, with Indiana on her lap, said to Celia, 'Can I tell you a joke?'

'Sure,' Celia answered.

'Okay. Knock-knock.'

'Who's there?' Celia replied.

'A talking dog,' said Aisha.

'A talking dog wh—' began Celia.

'WELL, HELLO THERE!' interrupted Indiana.

Celia's eyes nearly popped out of their sockets. 'Was that some kind of ventriloquist's trick?' she spluttered.

'No,' said Aisha, collapsing into a fit of giggles. 'We have a magic dog. Dad found him in a Scottish tomb.'

'But, shhh, please don't tell anyone,' said Indiana. 'I'm kind of a big hairy secret.'

'Promise?' Aisha said.

'Promise,' nodded Celia.

His gift now out in the open, Aisha and Indiana told them how the clues in Julimus's emails had led them to the library in Ephesus and all about what had happened underground. Dr Ghatak's eyes grew wide with pride when he heard of their meeting with the Lonely Avenger and Amie.

Indiana told them about the joy of meeting his mum, and how they were the connection

between the knight and Aisha. Then he told them proudly about his fabulous gift, being able to read fluently in a gazillion different languages.

Back in London, Julimus published details about Aisha finding the journal of the Lonely Avenger. It was, it turned out, the oldest book that had ever been found. As such, Aisha had a brief period of fame and was on the front pages of several newspapers, giving interviews about her adventures. Aisha kept all the magic bits a secret, of course – some things are better kept private.

During their holiday, Dr Ghatak hinted, several times, that there was more to Celia than met the eye, and that she had a secret

similar in scale to Indiana's, lurking just below the surface. This drove Aisha potty but her father was adamant he could say no more.

'Perhaps she really is a mountaineer,' said Aisha.

'Or an Olympic skateboarder,' joked Indiana.

'The owner of a theme park,' said Aisha, grinning back.

'Or the world's biggest ice cream shop!' they shouted together, collapsing into a fit of giggles.

'I can confirm that you're both as daft as each other, and not even close,' laughed Dr Ghatak. 'It is Celia's business and she will tell you when the time is right.'

The mystery cemented a blossoming

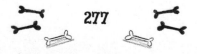

friendship between Aisha and Celia, and gave the whole family the sense that they were now a stronger team, who would be unwavering and relentless in their battle with the Serpent for the lost treasure of the Lonely Avenger.

I am excited already, and very much looking forward to telling you exactly how this whole funusual gladventure concludes.

Until then, my wonderful book potatoes, *ciao*.

I'll see you all very soon.

HH x

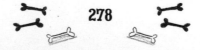

Discover more hilarious adventures
by Harry and Rebecca in the
Shiny Pippin series.